'A kiss is just a
Well, there's o

And before Morgan could back away Richard
Kavanagh's arms closed around her, and he
kissed her full on the mouth.

Morgan found her knees actually going weak
at this new assault on her senses; instinctively
she clutched at him for support. And at this
point, to her dismay, Morgan lost her head.
She took a sideways turn, drew her arm back,
and landed a powerful right jab on his eye.

Even now, nearly a year and a half later, she
cringed at the memory. It had been so uncool.
So unfeminine. Just about anything would
have been better than punching him.

He had laughed softly and seized hold of her
wrist. 'If I were you, I'd think about whether
I was so angry because I got something I
didn't want...' an index finger traced, with
casual contempt, her tingling mouth '...or
because I got more than I bargained for.'

Linda Miles was born in Kenya, spent her childhood in Argentina, Brazil and Peru, and completed her education in England. She is a keen rider, and wrote her first story at the age of ten when laid up with a broken leg after a fall. She considers three months a year the minimum acceptable holiday allowance but has never got an employer to see reason, and took up writing romances as a way to have adventures and see the world.

HEADING
FOR TROUBLE!

BY
LINDA MILES

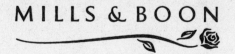

MILLS & BOON

MILLS & BOON and the Rose Device
are trademarks of the publisher.
Harlequin Mills & Boon Limited,
Eton House, 18–24 Paradise Road, Richmond, Surrey TW9 1SR

© Linda Miles 1996

ISBN 0 263 79483 0

Set in 10 on 11 pt Linotron Times
01-9605-59422

Typeset in Great Britain by CentraCet, Cambridge
Made and printed in Great Britain

CHAPTER ONE

AT FOUR-THIRTY on Good Friday afternoon Morgan Roberts stood halfway up a hill above Clive's Scrap and Lumber and wondered where she'd gone wrong.

She'd come down from London to spend Easter weekend with her father and young stepmother on the family farm near the Welsh border—surely a simple enough plan. But nothing in Morgan's life was ever simple.

Her decrepit alarm hadn't gone off, she'd thrown on the first clothes that had come to hand, raced across east London to Liverpool Street, chewed her nails— the Circle Line had been 'experiencing signalling problems'—and had almost missed her train out of Paddington. Not the best of starts. But she'd stepped demurely off the train three hours later filled with the very best intentions. Where *had* she gone wrong?

She'd meant to change the instant she got to the house, and here she was, three hours later, in a grey leotard which had once, long ago, been black, grey plimsolls which had once, long ago, been white, and a disreputable sarong which might, to an unsympathetic eye, have looked quite a lot like a recycled teatowel. She'd meant to behave with rigid conventionality from the word go, and instead. . .

'Go on, Morgan, you can do it!'

'It's *easy*!'

Sarah and Jenny, the nine-year-old Twins from Hell by her father's second marriage, took up a chorus they'd been repeating all afternoon.

'It's not scary!' Six-year-old Ben, the long-awaited son, added this with just a hint of a swagger.

5

Morgan tugged absently on the glossy black plait which had wormed its way over her shoulder like a confiding snake. A tender spring breeze rippled through young grass; the spring sunlight seemed to bathe the scene in champagne; it was a perfect afternoon for rolling down a hill inside a tyre. But she'd *promised* Elaine. . .

'This could be my chance of a breakthrough,' her sister had sighed over the phone earlier that week. 'No more breakfast TV for people who hate to get up in the morning. All right for some—they should try getting up in the middle of the night.'

Now Elaine had her eye on higher things—specifically on a place as co-host with Richard Kavanagh, the go-for-the-jugular presenter of *Firing Line*. There had been a short digression, which Morgan had heard dozens of times before, on his precocity, ratings, unheard-of salary and crazy fans—'Did you hear about the girl who smuggled herself into his hotel room in Carlisle?'—and then the axe had fallen.

'Someone from the studio's coming down from London this weekend,' Elaine had said mysteriously, refusing to name names, and had laid down the law in no uncertain terms. If Morgan didn't give the wrong impression by dressing in teatowels, jousting on broomsticks and otherwise disgracing herself, the job could be Elaine's for the asking.

'Aren't you going to try it even once?' asked Ben.

Morgan shook her head.

'It's got to go back to the scrapyard anyway,' Sarah said cunningly. 'What difference does it make if you're inside it?'

Morgan knew that she was being manipulated—it was well-known in the family that she never turned down a dare—but that didn't make it any easier to resist temptation. Elaine and the mystery guest weren't expected for hours—well, at least another hour. She looked longingly down at the inviting sand-hill at the foot of the slope, and sighed irritably.

She didn't care what Elaine said; she didn't really believe there could be a vacant seat on *Firing Line*. Morgan had met Richard Kavanagh only once, briefly, in circumstances that she would rather forget—but she considered herself something of an expert on his programme. Its coverage of controversial issues was undeniably addictive, and for the past three years she'd been getting weekly doses of the black-browed Boy Wonder of the box flaying alive the corrupt, the exploitative and the inefficient—but that didn't blind her to the ruthless showmanship of its sardonic presenter.

She couldn't see Richard Kavanagh taking on a co-host without a fight, and she couldn't see him taking on a fight without winning it, which meant that all her good behaviour was for nothing.

'Don't you like doing this kind of thing when you're grown-up?' Jenny asked guilelessly.

Morgan gritted her teeth. And then she remembered, suddenly, that Elaine hadn't said anything about *tyres*.

It was only five o'clock, anyway. Elaine would never know.

'Well, as a matter of fact I don't think Elaine would mind about tyres,' she said innocently, in a low, husky voice which gave grace to even her most casual remarks. The spark of mischief in her smoky grey eyes made her look more like a ten-year-old urchin than a five-foot-eight-inch twenty-six-year-old teacher. 'She didn't mention them.'

The children giggled delightedly.

Morgan settled herself inside the enormous, ex-articulated-lorry tyre, which she'd taken from the scrapyard just in case as being a better size for an adult. Pressing her elbows close to her sides, she gripped the inner rims of the tyre with her hands and took careful aim for the sand-hill. She gave a shove with her feet, tucking them quickly together as the tyre rolled forward. And she was off.

The tyre raced down the slope, turning over and over and over. Morgan's head swam as the world inside swept by in a revolving blur. There was a dull thud as the tyre struck the foot of the sand-hill; any second now it would keel over as it ran out of steam. But it didn't seem to be losing much speed.

The tyre rolled forward another foot or so, hesitated, and then began to roll down the other shoulder of the mound.

And now everything seemed to happen very fast. The tyre trundled briskly down the lane used by trucks for dumping sand, miraculously avoiding the ruts and potholes which might have stopped it. The gate at the end of the lane was open; the tyre cleared the crossroads at a single bound. It plunged, with stomach-churning abruptness, down the next slope, descended a pitted, rocky stream bed in a series of sharp, jarring bounces, soared over a drainage ditch at the foot of the hill and swept across the main road.

There was a scream of brakes.

The tyre took one final bound and came to rest in the marshy, rain-sodden ground below the road.

There was a blessed absence of motion. There was silence. And then there was the sound of a car door opening, and footsteps. Morgan extracted herself slowly, unsteadily from the tyre.

'Just what the *hell* did you think you were doing?' It was a man's voice, oddly familiar.

Morgan was now standing up to her calves in oozy mud—the same mud that was, she discovered, liberally plastered over the sarong, leotard and what she could see of her plait. She squelched forward, while the ground swayed and dipped and threw her to her knees in the mire.

'Are you all right?' he asked belatedly.

Morgan staggered to her feet again. She fixed her eyes on the stranger. Was it a stranger? The face was familiar. Sardonic, black-browed. . .

Morgan's head began to swim again. A voice inside it was saying, You idiot, you idiot, you *idiot*. Who else but fan-plagued Richard Kavanagh himself would *want* to keep his presence a secret? She should have known who Elaine's mystery guest would be—and, if she had, wild horses could not have dragged her where he might remember the last time they'd met.

Morgan didn't dare look at the car, where Elaine was no doubt waiting in icy rage. She looked down at the sarong; to say it looked like an old teatowel would have been to pay it a brass-faced compliment. She brushed ineffectually at a large clod of mud and grass, smearing it down the long line of her hip. What on earth was she going to do?

'Are you all right?' he repeated, adding, 'You bloody fool,' not so *sotto voce* for good measure. No, there was no mistaking him. Prudence might have suggested keeping her eyes down, giving him no chance to look her full in the face. Morgan raised her swimming head.

'Richard Kavanagh, I presume?' she said sarcastically, looking him straight in the eye. And she wondered dazedly what had hit her.

For the past three years she'd been shouting objections at the handsome, arrogant face whenever it had appeared on the screen; familiarity should long ago have robbed it of the power to surprise her. The black slash of brow, the eyes like burnished steel, the imperious, high-bridged nose and cynical mouth—features as much his trademark as the savage irony of his questions—were an undeniably potent combination, but she should have been used to them by now, for heaven's sake. She'd seen them probably *hundreds* of times—not exactly blind to their appeal, of course, but amused because they were so *obvious*.

Well, she wasn't laughing now. In the split second when their eyes met, the air between them seemed to crackle with electricity; she should have dragged her eyes away, but they seemed to have a will of their own. It was suddenly hard to breathe. And for what seemed an eternity but could only have been the space of a heartbeat she stared, enthralled, at the dark, piratical face gazing down at her.

In that instant of breathless concentration she was attuned to even his slightest change of expression—to the faint frown which greeted her cheeky remark, the sudden glitter when the brilliant eyes registered unerringly that swift spark of attraction.

Morgan could have sworn that she cared nothing for what Richard Kavanagh might think of her, but at his look of cold contempt she flinched violently—and struggled again for balance. And now the ill-used sarong seemed to feel that it had had enough; its knot parted, and it slid from her hips, down her long legs and into the mud, leaving a trail of slime in its wake.

The leotard covered rather more of her anatomy than the average swimsuit, but the look in Kavanagh's eyes made her feel as if she had stripped to the skin. She bent instinctively to retrieve the cloth from the mud.

The sudden movement was too much for her reeling head. Morgan swayed wildly from side to side, and at last fell headlong into his arms.

For an instant the world stopped pitching and heaving as she came to rest against a body which seemed to be all muscle. She was aware again, fleetingly, of that strange, uncomfortable breathlessness. And then her head began to swim again as Richard Kavanagh deliberately disengaged the hands which clutched at him. Hands like iron bands clasped her wrists and held her at arm's length. And as he steadied her the world came into focus again and Morgan stared at him in blank dismay.

On setting out for a weekend in the country, Richard Kavanagh had, she realised, done what most civilised adults would have done. He had changed before he'd left London so as to be presentable when he arrived. Specifically he had changed into a charcoal-grey linen jacket, grey trousers, a dark blue shirt and painted red silk tie—all of which were now streaked with mud and a green slime which clashed horribly with the colour scheme.

If she was honest she didn't give a brass farthing for the inconvenience to Mr Richard Kavanagh, but what on earth would Elaine say when she saw him?

'Oh, Mr Kavanagh, I'm terribly sorry!' she gasped. 'But I'm sure it will come out. If you'll let me have them I'll be happy to have them cleaned.'

'Oh, for God's sake!' In his exasperation he swung his arms wide, then in even greater exasperation caught hold of her again as she tilted sideways. 'It's very kind of you,' he said with withering sarcasm, 'but I'm actually rather attached to them. I didn't bargain on handing out souvenirs to the natives, so I'm afraid I only packed for one.'

Morgan stared at him uncomprehendingly. While she tried to gather her wits he proceeded to favour her with a trenchant condemnation of her manners, morals and intelligence with impressive fluency, not to mention a colourful vocabulary unrestrained by the decencies of the screen. After what seemed an hour, but could only have been a few minutes, he brought himself under control.

'I'm delighted that you like the programme,' he said very softly. He had stopped shouting, and there was somehow something even more unnerving in the sheer effort that went into confining himself to this silky, ironic tone. 'But I'm afraid that doesn't make me your personal property; and it certainly doesn't give you the right to endanger the lives of anyone who has the bad luck to be on the roads.

'Just out of curiosity I'd be interested to know exactly what you expected to get out of this ridiculous exhibition. Was I supposed to oblige you behind the nearest bush?' The grey eyes flickered over her in bored dismissal. 'Or were you just hoping I'd autograph the tyre?'

Morgan stared at him, open-mouthed. Of all the arrogant, conceited, self-satisfied. . . 'You think I'm one of your *fans*?' she said incredulously.

The cynical gaze showed not a flicker of self-doubt. 'Oh, were you hoping to break into television? I think you've picked the wrong industry, you know; perhaps you should think of Hollywood.' He paused, with the impeccable timing which made his style of interview so deadly. 'I've begged and pleaded for a casting couch, but the studio simply won't listen to reason.'

Morgan knew with maddening certainty that in half an hour she would have thought of twenty or thirty devastatingly witty replies with which to pulverise him. Now she could think of nothing but 'What?' and 'How dare you?'

'*What*?' she said, trying to make her venomous tone compensate for a certain deficiency in verbal brilliance. 'How *dare* you?'

He dropped her hands abruptly, and this time Morgan was steady on her feet. She felt as if she'd been nailed to the spot.

'Just one word of advice,' he said levelly. 'If you choose to act like a silly teenager, that's your own affair. But if you ever again pull a dangerous, irresponsible stunt like this to get my attention I'll give you something to remember me by all right, and I can guarantee you won't like it.' He gave her a singularly chilling smile and added pleasantly, 'If I were you I'd stick to coming up through cakes.'

He turned on his heel and walked back to the car. For all he knew, Morgan thought bitterly, she might have a concussion or worse, but he got into the car and slammed the door without a backward glance.

As she adjusted the muddy sarong about her hips again she did a sudden double take and looked again at the passenger seat—the *empty* passenger seat—of the car. Where was Elaine? And, come to think of it, why was he down here on the old canal road? The road to the house went out the other side of the village— this led only to the chemical processing plant and then back to the motorway.

A wild flash of hope seized her. Perhaps the appearance of Richard Kavanagh was sheer, devilish coincidence. Elaine had mentioned, she now remembered, that *Firing Line* was being pre-recorded for the bank holiday—but that would free other people from the studio besides its arrogant star. It defied belief that a consummate performer like Richard Kavanagh would willingly share the limelight; probably he had a team working on a programme in the area, and Elaine's mystery guest was part of the entourage. . .

Or someone higher up? Perhaps Elaine, at this very moment, was being driven along the motorway by a fat, bald TV executive—someone on whom Morgan still had a chance to make a good impression. A glance at her watch showed her just how slight a chance, and she scrambled back up the bank into the road.

The motor roared into life, and the car, which was now tilted down a slippery slope above the bog, began to reverse smartly and then slid another foot or so forward. There was an ominous gulping, sucking sound as the front tyres sank to the hub-caps in mud.

Morgan knew that she should feel sorry—after all, it was her fault, even if she hadn't meant to do it—but she couldn't help a mean satisfaction at this anticlimactic end to his grand exit. He might have had the last word, but he wasn't going to have the last laugh, she thought sourly.

The car's motor was cut off. Richard Kavanagh got out and began looking, not very hopefully, into the boot.

After a short struggle with herself Morgan squelched down the road to see if she could help.

'Go away,' he said, not looking up. 'If my car disappears under this swamp I plan to mark the spot with a human sacrifice, and I can't think of anyone I'd rather sacrifice than you. Why don't you get going now and put a safe distance between us while you've got the chance?'

Morgan searched for a snappy reply, failed to find one, and realised in exasperation that at least half her mind was taken up with the useless but distracting discovery that his rather raffish good looks were just as eye-catching seen in profile. 'Are you staying in the area?' she probed delicately. It seemed less of a dead give-away than, Where's Elaine?

'If there are many more like you around, not if I can help it. Now go away.'

'I *am* going,' said Morgan. 'I'm horribly late. I just wanted to say—'

'Unless you wanted to say you have a supply of two-by-fours up your sleeve I don't want to hear it. Scram.'

'What I wanted to say,' said Morgan, 'was that you need to get something under the tyres. There's a scrap and lumber-yard just up the hill.'

He turned his head now, flicking her an impatient glance—and as the diamond-hard eyes met hers unexpectedly Morgan's heart gave a queer little lurch. *Infuriating*. It wasn't as if she even *liked* the man—and he was obviously getting completely the wrong idea.

'And *also*,' Morgan added coldly, 'I am *not* one of

your fans. I think your interviewing methods are sadistic and self-serving and your looks make me think of a thirties matinée idol. I think you have about as much sex appeal as those Spanish bullfighters who think it proves their virility to kill an animal to entertain a crowd. I wouldn't give a bent paper-clip for one of your kisses, or for your signature, unless it was at the bottom of a cheque.'

'So this was more of an assassination attempt, is that it?'

'This was an accident,' she informed him haughtily. 'I was simply playing with the children and the tyre got away. It could have happened to anyone.'

'So that explains it,' said Richard Kavanagh, looking thoughtfully at the beached car. 'I was *wondering* why there were so many children around.'

'All right,' said Morgan. 'I made it up. Fine. I think I'll take my tyre back to the imaginary scrapyard and leave you to dream up something to brace your car with.' As she turned on her heel shrill cries drifted from above as the children peered down the slope to the main road. 'I've always had a very vivid imagination,' she remarked over her shoulder.

'All right, damn you,' said her sister's unsuspecting colleague-to-be. 'Remind me of where you imagined this bloody lumber-yard was.'

Which was probably, Morgan thought, Richard Kavanagh's idea of an apology. Not that she cared. If only he knew it, she was about to engineer his downfall. She would go back to the house and be amazingly charming and delightful to a fat, bald TV executive, and he would decide instantly that the sister of this wonderful person must appear on *Firing Line*. Little though Richard Kavanagh might suspect it, he was practically part of a double act already.

'Over there,' said Morgan, gesturing vaguely upwards. 'You can't miss it. I'd give you a hand but I'm horribly late. Good luck.' She looked up the hill, wishing that she could ditch the sarong for the climb—but she certainly wasn't going to with Richard Kavanagh watching. She strode resolutely to the foot of the slope.

'Wait a minute.'

Morgan turned back. 'Yes?' she asked coldly.

He glanced at his watch, then at the car, then with barely suppressed exasperation at Morgan. 'Are you sure you're in one piece? I've got a first-aid kit in the car if you need patching up,' he offered reluctantly.

'Oh, this is nothing,' Morgan said airily, unwisely shaking her head to emphasise the point. She staggered a step or two before catching her balance again.

'Do you need a lift somewhere?' he offered, even more reluctantly. 'If you don't mind waiting a few minutes. . .'

Morgan looked at the car, its nose tilted into the swamp. 'Thanks,' she said. 'But I don't think you're going my way.'

CHAPTER TWO

THE long, uncomfortable trek back to the house gave
Morgan plenty of time to cast a cold, self-critical eye
over her behaviour that afternoon. Her meeting with
Richard Kavanagh was, it seemed, only an accident;
she didn't think she'd hurt Elaine's chances *yet*. But if
she'd really taken Elaine's interests seriously she would
have been dressed and ready for company over an hour
ago. Well, she would make up for it all now, she vowed.
One bald, fat, cigar-smoking TV executive wouldn't
know what had hit him.

She left the children in the kitchen, vying to tell her
father and stepmother the story of her latest scrape,
and hurried upstairs to the room that she was sharing
with Elaine, her own having been made over to the
mystery guest.

Elaine's meticulously packed suitcase lay open on
one twin bed, but at least Elaine wasn't there. The
signs of her single-minded pursuit of success through
the years—the trophies and certificates and Elaine-
edited school newspapers, the photos of Elaine with all
the girls from the 'in' group at school—seemed to glare
at her in mute reproach as she tore off her wet, muddy
clothes, but at least it was better than hearing Elaine's
views of her carelessness at first hand.

She showered at breakneck speed, dried her hair,
managed to French-braid it on only the fifth attempt,
and at last slipped into the cherry-coloured silk tunic
that she had bought a few days earlier. 'Make an
effort,' Elaine had said, so she'd allowed herself to be
seduced by the blaze of embroidery, by the way the
superficial demureness of the princess collar, long,

17

close-fitting sleeves and knee-length hem was undercut by long slits up the sides of the skirt. Next she put on tights, new high-heeled shoes—must remember not to fall over, she thought—and then was ready for the *coup de grâce*.

Morgan examined rather nervously the collection of cosmetics that she'd bought, egged on by the mother of one of her pupils.

'Make the most of yourself,' Razna had urged, and had shown her how to apply lipstick and kohl, mascara and eyeshadow in a glamorous style which matched the dress.

Hastily Morgan did her best to follow the precepts she'd been given, lining her eyes with black, colouring her lips a brilliant crimson. At last she stood back and gazed doubtfully at her reflection. Striking, yes. Perhaps even beautiful. But the natural look it was not. Was this really what Elaine meant by making an effort?

Morgan hesitated, wondering whether she should just scrub it all off—she could imagine how her family would tease her. But in the mirror her eyes were great misty pools within their black rims, her mouth had a lovely bitter-sweet curve—how could you be too beautiful? She'd been enchanted by this unfamiliar image when Razna had first conjured it up, and surely a susceptible TV executive couldn't fail to be impressed?

Don't be such a coward, she told herself sternly. With an involuntary squaring of the shoulders she left the room and made her way precariously down the stairs and into the sitting room.

As the door opened a confusion of phrases burst upon her—'massive great tyre', 'dead easy', 'all afternoon', 'thought it was *safe*!' Her father and stepmother were nowhere to be seen. The room held the three children and Elaine, who sat on the sofa, one gleaming, silk-encased leg crossed over the other. Her suit of brilliant aquamarine raw silk, with its microscopic skirt,

made her look at once sexy and formidably self-
assured.

As Morgan came in Elaine pushed back the glossy
blonde hair which fell to her jaw in a sophisticated cut.
She shot Morgan a look which managed to convey both
exasperation over the afternoon's peccadillo and unen-
thusiastic assessment of her sister's clothes and make-
up.

Morgan suppressed a sigh. She should have known
that she couldn't carry it off. Well, at least the children
didn't know about Richard Kavanagh.

'You get more like Mother every day,' Elaine
remarked irritably. 'You know, the other day I saw a
piece in the paper — BRITISH TOURIST SETS OFF
AVALANCHE, ALPINE VILLAGE DESTROYED — and the first
thing I thought was, I didn't know Mother could ski.'

'I think she's in the Himalayas,' Morgan said noncommittally, fighting down an impulse to spring to her
mother's defence. Since their parents' divorce their
mother had been happily wandering remote corners of
the globe with little more than a pair of jeans and a
rucksack; twelve years later Morgan still sometimes felt
as if she'd lost her only ally.

'Well, God help Nepal,' Elaine said offhandedly.

Morgan changed the subject abruptly. 'Where's your
guest?' she asked, for there was no sign of the TV
executive who was to fall victim to her charms.

'I can't imagine,' said Elaine. 'He started well ahead
of me; I don't know what can be keeping him — Oh,
wait, that must be him now!'

From outside came the crunch of tyres on gravel. A
vague uneasiness plucked at Morgan; surely it was
impossible. . .?

They heard a door slam, footsteps. The doorbell
rang. Elaine fractionally adjusted her sleek, gleaming
legs and waited.

They heard their father hurrying up from the kitchen,

a door opening, muffled exclamations. Morgan could feel her heart pounding, as if it had slowed down while she'd held her breath.

A disjointed murmur grew gradually louder as Mr Roberts and his companion approached the door of the sitting room.

'The girls will look after you. You will forgive me, won't you? The Béarnaise sauce is at a frightfully *delicate* stage—'

Hasty footsteps retreated down the corridor, and the door opened on a tall, black-browed, sardonic man who bore not the faintest resemblance to the fat, cigar-smoking executive of Morgan's fond imagination.

For the second time that day Morgan's heart plummeted, and a voice in her head said, You idiot, you idiot, you idiot, you *idiot*.

'Richard, what on earth happened to you?' exclaimed Elaine. The newcomer also didn't look much like the cool, laid-back presenter of *Firing Line*. His hair was streaked with sweat, one black lock falling forward in his face, and, while he had taken off his jacket, his shirt and trousers were plastered with mud, as was the lower half of what had once probably been a nice tie.

'Had a spot of bother with a tyre,' he said offhandedly, with a crooked grin. 'Sorry to keep you waiting, but I'd better dash upstairs and change.'

'Of course,' said Elaine. 'I'll just introduce you quickly and then show you where we've put you. Let's see. . .this is Ben, Sarah, Jenny. . . Where's Morgan? Oh, there you are; and this is my sister Morgan. And, of course, this is Richard Kavanagh.'

He stared, eyes narrowed, at the brilliant creature who lurked in the corner.

'Well, look who's here!' he said. 'What a delightful surprise.'

Morgan looked at him dubiously, her black-rimmed

grey eyes wary. There was an odd little flutter in her stomach which made it hard to think straight—and she needed all her wits about her. She glanced nervously at Elaine.

'Do you two know each other, then?' asked Elaine. 'Oh, I suppose you must have met at one of my parties. What a memory you've got, Richard.'

Morgan remembered the brief, chilling glimpse she'd had of Richard Kavanagh at one of Elaine's parties and shuddered. All she needed was for him to remember it too. . .

'Is that where we ran into each other?' he asked her mockingly. Just for a moment Morgan felt a shameful, overwhelming relief—at least Elaine didn't *know* how badly she'd behaved. But then on the heels of relief came suspicion. He didn't miss much—he'd worked out that she didn't want Elaine to know about this afternoon. But he didn't owe her any favours. What kind of game was he playing?

'Oh, there are always so many people at Elaine's parties,' Morgan said vaguely. 'Lovely to see you again, anyway.' She gave him a bright, meaningless smile. 'Come on, kids; let's go and have dinner.'

Elaine looked surprised but not displeased. She'd bargained with Leah to have the children eat separately; the subtraction of Morgan from the grown-up table could only increase her chances of impressing her guest.

'Aren't you eating with us?' Morgan wasn't a bit surprised by his look of incredulity—he probably didn't think any female under the age of eighty would willingly forgo his company. She *was* surprised to see that he looked distinctly put out. He hadn't seemed all that anxious for her conversation an hour or so ago!

'Oh, it can be rather chaotic with this lot around; Leah thought you might prefer rational conversation,'

Morgan said airily. 'And I hardly ever get to see the children.'

'Why on earth should they be segregated just because of me?' he said, with an apparent modesty which made Morgan want to throw something—preferably at him. 'I know they must be starving, but I'll be back in half a tick—and then maybe we can work out where we met.'

Morgan caved in in the face of this veiled threat. For all the surface charm of his manner, there was a determination in the hard grey eyes which convinced her that further attempts to escape would be worse than useless. While Kavanagh disappeared upstairs she tried to think of a way of delicately warning Elaine— 'You remember your party the Christmas before last, the one where Richard Kavanagh walked into a door? I was the door'—and gave it up in despair.

He was back in twenty minutes, having changed into a white jacket and trousers and a pale green shirt, open at the neck. Morgan had grown up with boys who took it for granted that the tougher you were, the more torn and battered your clothes were; she found this combination of casual elegance and confident masculinity rather unnerving. While she was thinking about this Elaine walked up to Kavanagh and kissed him lightly on the mouth.

Morgan tried not to goggle. Was Elaine actually romantically involved with him, then? Or was this just one of those kisses that people in show business threw around as a casual social gesture?

Even as she puzzled it over, Kavanagh made it just slightly more than a gesture, if that was how it had been intended, by just barely bending his head, responding and at the same time fractionally lengthening the kiss. And somehow the very casualness of the embrace showed just how unquestionably these two handsome, stylish people belonged together—it was like watching Cary Grant kiss Grace Kelly.

'Sorry to keep you waiting,' Kavanagh murmured, while Morgan fought down a ridiculous sense of chagrin. As a child she had admired but not envied Elaine's golden-haired prettiness, priding herself instead on protecting the sister two years behind her, and on rivalling the boys for daring and toughness and complete indifference to clothes. But somehow daring and toughness didn't stand her in very good stead these days; somehow her sister's unabashed femininity gave Elaine an armour that Morgan couldn't hope to match.

Elaine made some offhand remark and they headed for the dining room. Morgan caught sight of herself in the mirror above the sideboard; her eyes were still misty pools, her mouth still had that wistful smile, but the lovely mask gave her none of the confidence she'd hoped for. She didn't *feel* feminine or glamorous; she felt a fraud who was about to be *un*masked at any moment.

This uneasy feeling was soon compounded, for the minute they sat down the children returned to that delightful subject—Morgan's escapades.

Leah ladled out soup, Morgan's father filled glasses, and the Terrible Twins launched yet again into the story of the tyre.

'Morgan's *always* doing that kind of thing,' boasted Jenny, with pride. 'She abseiled off the church tower for a bet—'

'And when Mick tried it he broke his arm!' burst in Sarah with the punchline.

'She went over the falls in a punt—'

'And Steve almost drowned!'

'She was in a motorcycle rally when she was fifteen!' said Ben, determined to get in this marvellous fact before one of the others did. 'And she jumped out of a parachute.'

'And lived to tell the tale,' said the visitor. 'Naturally.

I trust she visits the graves of Mick and Steve from time to time?'

Morgan glowered at him. A little smile was tugging at the corner of his mouth; he obviously thought that she was completely ridiculous. And then, just when she thought things couldn't possibly get any worse, her irritation gave way to horror as the children all but blew her cover.

'She jumped out of an *aeroplane, with* a parachute,' said Sarah. 'Ben gets *everything* wrong. And she raised seven hundred pounds for A Child's Place—isn't that wonderful?'

Morgan held her breath. The brilliant, penetrating grey eyes rested on her thoughtfully. 'Well, there's obviously a lot more to your sister than meets the eye,' he remarked in an ironical tone that made her want to hit him.

And then, to her dismay, he went on, 'Is A Child's Place some sort of charity, then? I don't think I've heard of it.'

'Morgan *teaches* there,' said Jenny. 'It's for poor little homeless children who don't have a school of their own.' She paused to admire the pathetic image conjured up by her words, and Richard Kavanagh pounced like a wolf—but not, of course, on the innocent little child who had spilled the beans.

'Surely there can't be much call for that?' he said. 'Anyone with a child has top priority for housing—'

'Yes,' said Morgan, who had been through this argument hundreds of times. 'But sometimes people get put in places that don't mesh very well with ordinary schools... We try to help children make the most of whatever time they have before they're moved somewhere else, instead of just expecting them to fit into a timetable set up to cover a whole school year, where if they fall behind it's just too bad—' She broke off, dismayed at where her enthusiasm was leading her. How much had he been told at that ghastly party?

'Yes, I see,' said Kavanagh. 'That makes much more sense—it's a good idea. I'm surprised no one has thought of it before; isn't anybody else doing anything?'

'No,' said Morgan.

'Are you sure? I seem to remember hearing of something very similar some time ago—I can't remember the name, but—'

'Why don't you put your research department onto it?' said Morgan. 'I'm sure if they dig around enough they can find someone to say it's completely superfluous. After all, there are two sides to every question, and if not you can always invent one just to be sure of being impartial.'

If she hadn't been so nervous she would have been amused by the look of blank astonishment which greeted this outburst. But before he could reply Elaine threw herself into the conversation with the aplomb of the experienced chat-show host, and for the next hour the talk remained firmly fixed on current events. Elaine's versatility on her breakfast show was nothing to the brilliance she showed now—she seemed to know about *everything*.

Morgan fought down another pang of regret at the contrast between her own gaucheness and Elaine's maturity. The whole point of having the man here was to give Elaine a chance to show her paces. She glanced down the table to see what sort of impression Elaine was making, and dropped her eyes hastily. He might be arguing with Elaine, but the cool grey gaze was still fixed unwaveringly on Morgan's face.

Just for an instant she felt a shameful, delicious frisson at his unexpected interest. But then cold sense pointed out the frightening, unflattering truth. He suspected something.

Presently she sensed that he had looked away, and

in spite of herself she found her eyes drawn slowly
back down the table. Sure enough, the hawk-like face
was now turned to Elaine. And now that she was no
longer the centre of attention she had the opportunity
to observe him at leisure.

Even after more than a year she remembered well
enough the contrast between the television image and
the real thing. The physical toughness of the man,
which you wouldn't have guessed from the talking
head, made it easier to understand how he had talked
his way into and out of a series of guerrilla hide-outs
for an early, notorious season of *Firing Line*. So, oddly
enough, did a charisma so strong that it was almost
palpable. She could imagine him impressing men who
lived by a code of unrelenting machismo—and then
charming the socks off them.

What she hadn't remembered, because she hadn't
previously had a chance to see it, was his rather
terrifying talent for being at ease with just about every
subject under the sun. Here he was, talking, unbriefed,
on subjects that Elaine had presumably worked up—
and still he had her on the hop.

But even as Morgan admitted, grudgingly, that he
probably had the most powerful mind of anyone she'd
ever met, even as she laughed, reluctantly, at his
irreverent wit at the expense of the world's movers and
shakers she found herself gritting her teeth.

Again and again he deployed the same tactic, putting
forward a controversial, even shocking suggestion 'for
the sake of argument', and then leaving Elaine to
struggle to show why it was wrong. When watching this
move on television Morgan usually shouted at the
screen. Now, while her sister fought off humiliation at
the hands of a man she seemed to care about personally
as well as professionally, Morgan was forced to keep a
low profile, to open her mouth only to put peas into it.

While she managed to keep quiet, however, it didn't

occur to her to school her face to an air of pleasant interest, and it gradually settled into a stormy expression strangely at odds with the harem-like make-up. Kavanagh glanced her way from time to time with a rather odd smile, and once or twice tried to draw her into the discussion; each time she made a noncommittal remark, her eyes still hurling defiance, and refused to be drawn.

But at last it was too much to bear. He had been talking with chilling satisfaction about a prominent local politician whose corruption had been exposed by *Firing Line*, and who was now serving time in a low-security prison. Morgan glared at him.

His eye caught hers for a long moment. 'But you seem to disapprove?' An eyebrow flickered upwards; a lazy smile mocked her for daring to disagree.

'I thought it was absolutely appalling, the way you took Corvin to pieces,' she said, goaded. 'Why did you have to keep needling him about his sixties idealism? He looked absolutely heartbroken by the end of the programme. What possible good did it do?'

He gave a faint, indifferent shrug. 'He got the post in the first place because he persuaded people that he'd be an improvement on the back-scratching lot who'd been running it for twenty years. It seemed fair enough to bring that up if he'd turned into something as bad as what he was meant to replace.'

This was as good as a red flag to a bull. Morgan forgot her promise to be tactful and discreet and behave like a civilised adult; how dared he pretend that he only brought up legitimate points, when he really just played to the crowd? Infuriated, she sailed in with a comprehensive list of every disgraceful bit of show-manship she could remember.

'And what about Cy Burgess?' she concluded. 'Or Everard Macready? What about the time you read out letters that union leader—what was his name? Mick

Bryson?—had written to the wife of the owner of FairWay? Was that necessary? I suppose you thought it was absolutely marvellous when he actually passed out on stage.'

The electric grey eyes widened as she went on, and by the time she had finished his clever, mobile face showed an odd mixture of emotions—surprise, amusement, perhaps a touch of respect, but above all a maddening self-satisfaction. Remorse, it seemed, was conspicuous by its absence.

'Morgan,' he said at last, 'as far as I can see you've caught just about every broadcast of the programme for the last three years—and that despite loathing everything about the way I go about things.'

He cocked an eyebrow. 'I hate to say this, but as far as I'm concerned that means I must be doing something right. For better or worse, that's what television's about—not just covering worthy issues, but getting people to watch you week after week after week.' His mouth curled into a rather cynical smile. 'Whatever you say about my methods, if you keep watching I must be doing a pretty good job.'

'But don't you personally have any opinion of whether it's right to treat people that way?' Morgan demanded. 'What do you do—give them all an apology and a pat on the back afterwards—no hard feelings, it was just business? That may be good enough for the Godfather, but don't you think you should come up with something better if you're going to take the moral high ground?'

He began to look slightly annoyed. 'I try to make sure of my facts; assuming I've got those right, I don't think what I say calls for apology. That doesn't mean I have a licence to insult people at will; if I get hold of the wrong end of the stick, of course I offer a retraction.'

Morgan scowled.

'For God's sake, you can't seriously think I do it for the sheer fun of being rude to people?' His voice roughened with impatience.

'Of course you enjoy it!' Morgan retorted. 'You *love* twisting the knife—and *some* people love to watch you do it, though why I can't imagine. It may be good TV, but don't you ever wonder whether the kind of spectacle you provide limits the stories you can cover? No—because you *revel* in hacking people apart.'

There was a stunned silence around the table. Mr and Mrs Roberts looked shocked, the children thrilled, Elaine gallantly cheerful, as if one of her morning TV guests had passed out in a drunken stupor. Only Richard Kavanagh seemed unfazed. If anything, he looked more animated than he had all evening. The queer light eyes positively blazed under the black brows, and a smile tugged at his mouth.

'I like to think my weapon is the rapier,' he murmured. And then, with an apparent shift of ground, he added, 'But I'm quite capable of taking an interest in subjects and people where there's not a hint of wrongdoing.'

He smiled. 'Look, sterling probity may not make for very interesting TV, but that's not to say it doesn't exist, *or* that I'm incapable of appreciating it when I find it—you may not have noticed, but just at the moment I'm not actually on the air.' And then, while Morgan tried to think of a polite way of saying, Tell that to the Marines, he slid his blade home.

'So why don't you tell me a bit more about your work with the poor little homeless children with no school of their own?' The amusement in his voice invited her to share the joke, but this home thrust stopped Morgan in her tracks.

'I'd be happy to,' she lied. 'When we've more time.'

'It's so nice to have the chance to meet fans face to face,' he said lazily, 'and find out what they really

think.' The fist inside the velvet glove, thought Morgan;
he was threatening to let Elaine know what she'd been
up to. But her scrape of this afternoon paled to
insignificance beside the mess she'd be in if he remembered where he'd seen her before, or, for that matter,
decided to take a real interest in the charity.

'I didn't think you had much time for your fans,' she
replied coolly. 'After all, I don't suppose you care for
being treated as somebody's personal property.' She
met his eyes squarely, daring him to take up the
gauntlet.

'That,' he said mildly, 'depends very much on the
person.' And he gave her an outrageously charming
smile.

Morgan made the interesting discovery that a smile
could have all the impact of a punch in the solar
plexus—even when you were actually furious with the
owner. The man was a public menace; she could feel
her resistance crumbling, could actually feel the corners
of her own mouth turning up in involuntary response
to that look of extravagant admiration. It didn't even
seem to matter that she *knew* it was an act—she knew
how ridiculous she must look beside Elaine, and *still*
she felt herself warming to him.

She bit her lip fiercely and glared at him. He was
here to be impressed by Elaine, not to flirt with Elaine's
sister.

'Are you finished with your plate?' she asked
abruptly. While they had been scrapping everyone had
finished eating. Escape was at hand.

Morgan turned to her stepmother. 'You've been
slaving for hours, Leah, and tomorrow will be just as
bad. Go and lie on a sofa somewhere,' she said firmly.

She stood up and began collecting the rest of the
dishes and carrying them out to the kitchen.

Chairs scraped in the dining room; she could hear
people moving towards the front room. Alone at last!

'Here, let me give you a hand,' said a voice behind her.

Morgan realised too late that she had walked into a pit of her own digging. But how could she have guessed that the monster killer ego would condescend to help with the washing-up? And now, just when she needed to think on her feet, that strange, stupid breathlessness had come back and she was distracted by an uncomfortable consciousness of his closeness.

The deep, drawling voice had spoken almost in her ear, and as she whipped around automatically to face him she found that they were only inches apart. Unbidden, the thought flashed through her mind that Elaine, raising her mouth to kiss him, had stood no closer than she was now. And she was taller than Elaine.

What on earth was the matter with her?

'Don't be silly; you're a guest,' she protested, backing away hastily.

'I try to be a good one,' he replied virtuously, and laughed at her sceptical look.

'But you should be—that is, wouldn't you rather talk to Elaine?' Morgan began nervously stacking dishes in the sink and allowing hot, soapy water to rise around them.

'Ah, Elaine. I take it that dazzling performance was for my benefit? Don't look so horrified, Morgan; I said it was dazzling, didn't I? More credit to her for making an opportunity for herself. But I can't, offhand, think of a tactful way of telling her to consider herself auditioned, so I thought I'd come out here and make myself useful.'

'Naturally you wouldn't *dream* of saying anything that might cause offence,' said Morgan.

'Well, not without a studio audience,' he said shamelessly. 'Why don't you let me wash while you dry, since you know where everything goes?' His voice was not precisely gloating, but there was no doubt about it—he

certainly thought that he'd won this round hands down.
And now he had her where he wanted her—over the
washing-up he would give her the kind of grilling which
had tripped up people who were cleverer, wilier and
more experienced at downright lying than she would
ever be. Unless. . .

Morgan's eyes swept rapidly round the kitchen.
'Wash as you go' was not a precept that Leah had ever
taken to heart; every surface was piled high with pots,
pans, mixing bowls and every conceivable implement
which could be used in the preparation of a dinner for
eight. The sink was now filled with the dinner dishes,
as was the counter beside it. And this scene of chaos
had given her an idea of breathtaking simplicity—and,
it had to be said, outrageous bad manners. But at least
it would save her from a tête-à-tête with Richard
Kavanagh.

Morgan took a deep breath. She looked resolutely
into the soapsuds; she didn't dare look up at him. 'It's
awfully nice of you,' she said. 'Are you *sure*?' It was
still not too late to back out.

'Quite sure.' He had tossed his jacket over the back
of a chair and was already rolling up his sleeves. There
was probably a warning somewhere in the contrast
between his casual, trendy clothes and the lean muscle
of the arms being laid bare; Morgan ignored it. So he
thought he'd outflanked her, did he?

'Well, if you insist,' said Morgan, stepping away from
the sink. She raised limpid eyes to his face. 'We always
leave things to drain,' she explained in a matter-of-fact,
helpful tone of voice. 'It's more hygienic than drying
with a dish towel. You can just leave everything in the
rack. Thanks very much for offering; I *have* had rather
a long day. It's *terribly* nice of you.' She managed to
meet his eyes with a straight face.

Once out of the kitchen, she stumbled down the hall,
doubled over with laughter, hands clapped to her

mouth, until she staggered at last to the coat-rack, buried her face in a coat, and howled.

When she had herself under control—more or less under control—Morgan returned to the sitting room to join the rest of the family.

'Where's Richard?' asked Elaine in a discontented tone.

'Oh, he insisted on doing the washing-up,' Morgan said cheerfully.

'*What*?'

'He wouldn't take no for an answer,' Morgan added smugly.

'Oh, my *God*,' said Elaine in horror. 'Well, I'd better go and give him a hand.' She hastened out of the room.

And now, for the first time that evening, Morgan was able to relax. But as she picked up a magazine and leafed idly through it she was suddenly, wryly, aware of a faint sense of anticlimax.

She had actually got the better of Richard Kavanagh! But the problem was she couldn't be there to savour her victory—to see his face as he tackled the washing-up, or was joined by Elaine, keen to score a few more points over the soapsuds. And, even worse, she found herself actually looking forward to his return from the kitchen. He wasn't the kind to take defeat lying down; what would he do next?

Morgan reminded herself sternly that she wasn't supposed to be crossing swords with him at all. In fact, looking back over the evening, she couldn't understand what had got into her—she had meant to be so quiet and unobtrusive! She had *promised* Elaine to act conventionally. Where had it all gone wrong?

An image came to her of cool grey eyes, amusement lurking in their depths. He *made* me do it, she protested to herself. He deliberately set out to thwart me at every turn; was I supposed to take that lying down? And as for keeping him company in the kitchen... An older,

more sinister image came to her—of those same grey
eyes glittering in winter moonlight. . .

Everything he'd said at dinner showed that he hadn't
changed; the merciless predator who took pleasure in
the hunt wasn't far beneath the surface. She *had* to
keep him from remembering her, and keep him from
going anywhere near A Child's Place. But that was no
reason, she reminded herself, to jeopardise Elaine's
chances. As long as he stayed she must simply keep out
of his way. From now on she would have to do better.

CHAPTER THREE

'TELL me the story of Gareth again, Morgan.'

Morgan looked up from her unread magazine an hour later to find Ben standing beside her. 'I can't watch TV 'cos Sarah and Jenny are watching *The Little Mermaid*,' he explained.

Morgan grinned at this flattering invitation. The little boy climbed onto the sofa beside her, and the two were soon lost in the story of the humble kitchen boy who came to the aid of a haughty lady. Each time the boy defeated a knight in battle the lady exclaimed that it was luck, and a shameful thing that a brave knight should be brought low by a dirty kitchen boy. And about a third of the way into the story the hairs rose on the back of Morgan's neck, and she knew that Richard Kavanagh had come into the room.

She forced herself not to look up. Gareth defeated a red knight, a green knight, a blue knight, a black knight and a giant, and still the lady despised him. From the corner of her eye Morgan saw a pair of white-trousered legs prop themselves against a table, the scrubbed cotton taut over the long, lean muscle of his thighs.

'And then he returned to the court of King Arthur and jousted in disguise, and defeated every knight who came at him, even Sir Gawain,' she said, her voice even huskier than usual from nervousness. She could just imagine what Kavanagh would make of this. 'And then he went to the king and said, "I am the brother of Gawain, but I wished to be made a knight for my own efforts, and not because of my brother." And he was knighted that very day, and Sir Gareth married the lady and lived happily ever after,' she concluded hastily.

The silence at the end of this seemed to stretch out interminably. At last, in spite of herself, Morgan's eyes were drawn slowly up to the face of the man watching her.

She had expected to see the spark of devilry which had been lurking in his eyes all evening, perhaps anger, certainly the promise of vengeance to come. But the hawkish face had an expression of almost brooding intensity; it was impossible to believe that its bitter cynicism had been prompted by anything so trivial as being unexpectedly landed with the washing-up.

His eyes held hers for an endless moment in which she was conscious only of the pounding of her heart, of the electric charge which seemed to strike her from those quicksilver, black-rimmed irises. And when he spoke his words took her completely by surprise.

'That's Malory, isn't it?' he asked, in a casual tone which made her wonder if she'd imagined that sombre look. 'Tennyson misses the point—can't see why anyone would want to get by on his own merits, so he makes the disguise a whim of the boy's mother, isn't that right?'

'Yes,' said Morgan. Her eyes fell to the pale green shirt, which had got splashed just above the belt and had grease-spots up the front, and some devil prompted her to add, 'Do you have a fellow-feeling for Gareth, then, Mr Kavanagh?'

'Oh, he had the right idea; I'm dead against people rising through their connections,' he replied, and then added more cynically, 'Though it was lucky for him that Arthur wasn't one of the bad guys, wasn't it? But perhaps I'm biased, speaking as one who got his start doing an exposé of the Round Table.' With an abrupt change of gear, he went on, 'Do call me Richard, though. Or is that your way of saying you'd rather I didn't call you Morgan?' And suddenly the gleaming spark of devilry was back.

'You've called me worse things,' said Morgan drily, with heroic self-restraint.

'I know, damn it.' He ran a hand absently through his hair. 'I want to talk to you.'

Morgan bit her lip. 'I'd love to,' she said insincerely. 'But it's way past Ben's bedtime. Perhaps some other time.' She stood up abruptly, dislodging Ben briefly before gathering him up onto her hip.

At once her adversary rose to his feet as well, blocking off her path to the door. Looking up reluctantly, Morgan saw that one rebellious lock of hair had fallen forward onto his face, giving him an almost boyish look—but there was nothing boyish about the intent determination of the face bent towards her.

He had only just turned thirty, she remembered; if he had accomplished so much so young, it was because he was completely ruthless. Ruthless and not to be trusted. But even as she thought it his eyes lit with amusement, and his mouth curled in a smile that tempted her to respond.

'Are you avoiding me because of this afternoon?' he murmured, in an intimate voice pitched so low that she had to force herself not to move closer to hear him. 'I wanted to make amends—honest.' The grey eyes flashed her another gleaming glance. 'But I thought I'd be discreet.'

Looking up into the cynical, charming face, so confident of an easy victory, Morgan realised bitterly that there was no justice in the world. If it hadn't been for Elaine, how much she would have enjoyed this conversation!

She could just imagine what Richard Kavanagh would have done to a celebrity who had nearly knocked someone down, assumed she was after him, and abandoned the innocent victim at the scene of the accident—*he* wouldn't have let someone off the hook just because he said he was sorry. How she would love to give him a taste of his own medicine! What exquisite revenge she could take for the mortification of their first meeting! And instead. . .

'I'm not avoiding you,' she said stolidly. 'It's just time to take Ben up to bed.'

His eyes began to dance. 'Well, perhaps I could give you a hand?'

As Morgan searched desperately for an excuse she saw, furiously, that he was actually *enjoying* her predicament. Well, he wasn't going to corner her so easily again. 'Oh, no, Richard, I couldn't let you do that,' she said sweetly. 'You've done far too much tonight already.' She gazed up at him with an expression of wide-eyed, glowing gratitude. 'I really don't know how to thank you.'

For a moment she wondered whether she'd gone too far. There was a startled silence as he registered the fact that she was actually baiting him in return. And then, maddeningly, his eyes blazed up, not with anger, but with the delight of someone who had discovered that a game had surpassed all expectations. His eyelids drooped over the glinting eyes; one eyebrow shot up. 'I can think of a few ways,' he said. 'You must let me tell you about them some time.'

Morgan blushed furiously. Where was Elaine? Why wasn't she here showing off her knowledge of the exchange rate mechanism or some similarly incomprehensible subject, instead of throwing her sister to the wolf? In exasperation she pushed past him, trying not to flinch as she brushed against him.

He laughed softly. 'You can't run away from me for ever, Morgan,' he told her. 'I always get what I want, sooner or later.'

Morgan stalked out of the room.

* * *

By the time she had tucked Ben in it was still only
nine-thirty. Morgan wasn't about to go downstairs with
the wolf still on the prowl; she would read in bed. She
returned to Elaine's room to take off her bright clothes,
then slipped into the extra-large Child's Place T-shirt
which was her current nightgear.

She paused for a moment by the mirror, a frown
creasing her brow. Her attention was caught, not by
the wide-eyed houri who gazed at the glass, nor by the
long, almost coltish legs which remained largely
uncovered by the T-shirt, but by the new logo, the new
name, and the new slogan—'There's no place like it'—
each of which was rumoured to have cost several
thousand pounds from a top agency.

Madness, she thought irritably, exasperated for the
thousandth time by the charity's prodigal expenditure
on its image—and the marketing strategy was no better.
You had only to look at the hundreds of designer T-
shirts stacked in the storeroom to see why cash flow
was a problem, why the director so often rejected even
modest applications for classroom supplies. Or, for that
matter, she thought cynically, to see why Ruth refused
point-blank to let her look at the accounts!

Morgan had spent two years after she'd left university founding and making a success of a specialist cake
firm. She'd decided that she would rather work with
children than turn a small business into a large one,
and had never regretted the change—but what she'd
heard about the management of the charity made her
itch to get her hands on it. The problem was that no
one paid any attention to a teacher.

Morgan tugged absent-mindedly on the end of her
plait. Even the underfunded classroom she ran was
better than anything else available to the children. But
it would be easy enough to hold the place up to ridicule;
she could just imagine Richard Kavanagh standing in

the overstocked storeroom making sarcastic comments while supporters deserted in droves.

He wouldn't care what happened to the children—all he cared about was good TV. And if he remembered a certain embarrassing incident at a Christmas party. . .

Morgan shuddered. The worst of it was, she thought uneasily, that he might well feel that the last few hours had given him a few more debts to pay off. Well, she would just have to dodge him for another two days, before he remembered he had a score to settle.

She was on the point of going to the bathroom to clean her teeth when a sudden, horrible thought occurred to her. So far he hadn't connected the unfamiliar name with the organisation he'd heard of at that fateful party. But just avoiding him wouldn't keep him in the dark for long when her old room was crammed with the old material. The unmemorable LECDC—London Educational Centre for Displaced Children—might not ring a bell with him, but she wouldn't bet on it. There was no help for it; she would have to get them out at once.

With a little shrug she walked rapidly down the corridor to her own room.

There was no light beneath the door; it was only quarter to ten, after all, and there was no reason to expect anyone upstairs for at least another hour. Morgan slipped into the room. Most of the materials should be on the desk; feeling somehow safer with the light out, she felt her way cautiously across the floor.

Just as she reached the desk she heard footsteps in the corridor. There was no way that she could escape with the damning literature; hastily she pulled open the bottom drawer, thrust the stack of papers firmly down in it and slammed it shut. The door opened and a sliver of light cut the darkness.

'I'm sorry about the washing-up, Richard—we don't usually work our guests quite so hard.' Morgan couldn't see Elaine, but the tone of slightly forced amusement gave her some idea of the reckoning in store for her—and that was if Elaine *didn't* discover her lurking half-dressed in Kavanagh's room. Morgan held her breath; the voice in her head seemed to be too disgusted even to say, You idiot.

'That's all right; I was glad to have a chance to hear some of your ideas.' At least the door hadn't opened wider—he didn't seem to be bringing Elaine in. 'Goodnight, Elaine.'

There was quite a long pause before Elaine replied, 'Goodnight, Richard.' It didn't take much imagination to guess what had filled it.

Then Elaine's footsteps retreated. The door opened wider, and the light came on. Morgan stood blinking in the glare. There was a short silence.

'Well, well,' said Richard Kavanagh. 'Alone at last.'

He closed the door quietly behind him.

There was a watchful look in his eyes. Morgan remembered suddenly the story that Elaine had told her about the girl at the hotel and found herself blushing furiously. What on earth could he think? She scowled at him defiantly, daring him to think the obvious.

'This is actually my room,' she said awkwardly, uncomfortably aware that the T-shirt seemed to be a lot shorter than it had been when she'd put it on. 'I'm sharing with Elaine. I just wanted to get a few things before you came up.'

'I see.' His face was unreadable. 'Sorry. I hadn't realised you'd been put in with Elaine to give me a room for myself.'

Morgan detected a criticism of the sleeping arrangements in this remark, and sprang automatically to Elaine's defence.

'I hope you don't mind being put in my room,' she

said apologetically. 'Leah is rather conservative, and she doesn't—er—'

'Like people doing the dirty deed under her roof?' he completed helpfully.

'No! That is—'

'Never mind, I get the picture. Raving sex maniac that I am, I'll naturally have to endure agonies of frustration—'

Morgan was surprised to detect a note of annoyance in his voice. 'I never said that,' she protested. Why on earth was he being so prudish all of a sudden? *He* was supposed to be the sophisticated one. *He* was the one who'd just been kissing Elaine outside the door.

'You implied something very like it.' He thrust his hands into his pockets. 'To tell the truth, it never occurred to me that we might share a room,' he added offhandedly. 'Do you think Elaine expected it?'

'No, but—'

'You thought it up all by yourself. How kind.'

Morgan reminded herself that she had promised Elaine to behave like a civilised adult. Civilised! She'd like to black his eye. Her right hand automatically curled into a serviceable fist; she forced it open again. *No.*

'I'm sorry to have barged in,' she said in a carefully controlled voice. 'I'll clear out now.'

There was a short pause, and when he spoke again she had the impression that he too had been reminding himself of the demands of civilised behaviour.

'No, don't go,' he said, and he began to move towards her, the spark of devilry very bright in his eyes. 'We've some unfinished business.'

He'd remembered. Morgan stared at him in horror. 'H-have we?' she stammered.

'Of course.' He paused automatically, with his familiar and maddening instinct for timing, then added, 'I wanted to apologise for this afternoon, remember?'

With the rush of relief came anger. How dared he torment her and then turn around and pretend to be polite? 'But you already have,' said Morgan guilelessly.

'What? When?' he asked, startled.

'This afternoon,' she replied instantly. 'You said, "All right, damn you," when you saw the children. I distinctly heard you.'

His eyes met hers for an electric moment, and then, to her astonishment, he laughed out loud—not the short, cynical laugh which was his stock-in-trade, but an unpremeditated shout of laughter which seemed to involve the whole of that long, lean body. The grey eyes, meeting hers, seemed to sparkle with delight.

'Where have you been all my life?' he asked, grinning. 'I did very handsomely admit to being in the wrong, now you come to mention it—but let's say I feel I owe you a more conventional apology. Do you forgive me?'

'Yes,' said Morgan.

He did not seem entirely satisfied by this. 'I know I overreacted—there's something about persecution by fans that brings out the worst in one. I don't know how the real superstars stand it year in year out; as far as I'm concerned, the past couple of years have been absolute hell, never knowing when some fool of a woman is going to do something perfectly idiotic—'

He broke off, and gave her a rerun of the charming smile. 'Sorry, I don't mean that the way it sounds. The worst of it is it makes every other woman think you must have a swollen head—that you must go round expecting every woman you meet to fall flat on her back the moment you say hello.'

Morgan found that she was literally grinding her teeth at this self-congratulating excuse for an apology. What a charlatan the man was! Was she really supposed to fall for this? Answer—yes, like a ton of bricks.

'Oh, I'm sure you'd buy a girl a drink,' she said, suppressing several pithy replies.

'Or even two,' he agreed imperturbably. 'I must say you're taking it very well.'

'Well, I didn't take it very seriously,' she said. 'After all, it's just what you do on your programme all the time. If I'd been a fan I'm sure it would have given me a terrific thrill to see the real thing.' Her amused, husky voice endorsed his dismissal of the idiocy of fans. 'Let's forget all about it,' she added magnanimously.

'It's not quite what I do on my programme...' he began, with a slight edge to his voice.

'I know,' Morgan said sympathetically. 'Censorship is such a nuisance.' She closed her lips tightly on the little bubble of laughter that came on the heels of the words.

Again he surprised her by laughing. 'You don't know how much,' he agreed. 'You little devil, you're enjoying this, aren't you? And, come to think of it, you've already had your pound of flesh. If you could have seen your face in the kitchen! Mouth as prim as pie, and those great, wicked eyes laughing at me. "It's *terribly* nice of you,"' he mimicked in a saccharine falsetto.

'But Richard,' protested Morgan, smiling in spite of herself, 'you *insisted*.' And at his roar of laughter she found herself helplessly joining in.

'More fool me,' he said at last, when he had stopped laughing. 'Morgan, why don't you come out with me tomorrow? I've got some digging around to do—come along and hold a spade and I'll buy you lunch.'

She sobered abruptly as she realised how completely she had lowered her guard. How did he *do* it? In the space of something like five minutes he'd turned the situation on its head. The fact was that he'd neatly cut the ground from under her feet, making it almost impossible for her to keep him at a distance—but she hadn't even noticed. The laughter in those brilliant eyes had gone to her head like champagne—and for one insane moment, she realised in disgust, she'd actually been tempted to accept.

Well, she'd always wondered how he kept up the supply of victims on *Firing Line*, and now she knew: however often people had seen the kind of treatment they could expect, they probably thought it would be different for them. But the fact was that this was just part of the game. The jokes were neither here nor there; if he thought you had something to hide you could expect no mercy.

'I'm afraid I've already made plans for tomorrow,' she said. For a moment she thought that he was about to ask what plans but, if he was, he managed to keep his interviewing instincts under control.

'Well, how about a goodnight kiss to show there are no hard feelings?' Two strides brought him to her; one hand rested on her shoulder, the other cupped her chin.

Morgan glared up at him. 'I'm not quite ready to fall on my back yet,' she said sarcastically. 'And I don't come when you snap your fingers, either. In words of one syllable, I am not one of your fans.'

He looked taken aback, one bold black eyebrow shooting up in surprise. She would have liked to think it was just another example of his arrogance—assuming that she would want to be kissed by him—but it was probably sheer astonishment at her unsophisticated reaction to something he took so casually.

'Congratulations,' he said. 'People hardly ever do use words of one syllable when they say "in words of one syllable". Have you noticed?' He bent his head; his lips brushed her cheek. A faint scent—an oddly potent mixture of freshly washed cotton, male skin and the citrus of washing-up liquid—tantalised her nostrils, and then it was over.

'Just to show there are no hard feelings,' he repeated,

straightening up and dropping his hands in his pockets. 'For sinking my car in a swamp, leaving me to wash every piece of crockery in five counties, and making me out to be the worst thing since the Spanish Inquisition. Want to slap my face for taking liberties?'

'Don't be ridiculous,' said Morgan.

'Disappointed?'

'Of course not.' Her face tingled as if an electric current had been sent through it.

'Liar.' He grinned. 'I won't suggest you reciprocate, anyway—I could have sworn you didn't give a damn about this afternoon, but there's no reason why you should make empty gestures if it sticks in your craw. I know I've a filthy tongue sometimes, and I don't mean just four-letter words.'

Morgan detected genuine self-reproach in his voice this time and was instantly stung by pangs of guilt. She hadn't really cared about all the insults he'd heaped on her—and, as for the bad language, she knew seven-year-olds who could have taught him a thing or two. She couldn't even fuel her indignation at his sexual presumption, since it seemed that he hadn't meant to make a pass at all.

'Of course I don't care about this afternoon,' she said, and impulsively, without giving herself time to think about it, she put one hand behind his neck to pull his head forward and kissed him lightly on the cheek.

This time the shock ran through her mouth and the tips of her fingers. She stepped back in confusion, as if he could actually tell what she felt—but surely she wasn't that transparent?—and said hastily, trying to cover up with a joke, 'Anyway I suppose it's a compliment in a way. I mean, you did say I should sell my body in Hollywood. But perhaps you say that to all the girls.'

'Only if they've got the figure for it,' he said instantly. She'd already worked out that flirting came as naturally to him as breathing, but in spite of his smile there was a look in his eyes which she didn't like—the keen, probing look of someone confronting a problem that did not make sense. 'It's sweet of you to put my mind at rest, Morgan,' he said in the slow, drawling voice which was used to such devastating effect on *Firing Line*. 'And I'm naturally glad to hear I haven't mortally wounded you. But if you didn't mind about this afternoon, why the hell *have* you been avoiding me?'

And as he waited, arms folded, one eyebrow raised, Morgan saw to her fury that he had trapped her yet again. How could she have been such a fool as to take him at face value? Hadn't she seen just this manoeuvre on *Firing Line* more times than she could count—the awkward question apparently dropped, the victim allowed to move on, only to find the neglected point explode in his face like a time bomb?

'Is there something else I don't know about?' he persisted. '*Have* we met before?'

'I'm sure I'd remember if we had,' she said truthfully.

'So why do you keep running away?'

'Why won't you leave me alone?' Morgan retorted in exasperation.

He laughed softly. 'Do you really need me to explain that?'

Morgan stared at him. Did he mean that he knew after all? Was he playing a cat-and-mouse game? Or was he just trying to trick her into giving herself away? He was notorious for his ruthlessness in dealing with evasive opponents. Well, she was not about to hang around and see it at first hand.

'I'm not avoiding you,' she said, backing towards the door. 'You're imagining things.' She opened the door. 'Goodnight, Richard,' she said firmly, and bolted into the corridor, closing the door behind her.

Unfortunately her retreat to her own sleeping quarters only threw her directly in the path of Elaine, who had come upstairs in search of blood. She sat on the edge of her bed, one leg crossed over the other, swinging a foot ominously.

'Are you out of your mind, Morgan?' she demanded as soon as Morgan opened the door. 'How could you come down looking like that?'

Morgan's heart was still pounding from her narrow escape. She made an effort to collect herself. 'You said I should make an effort with my appearance,' she protested feebly.

'I never said you should look like Mata Hari,' Elaine said bitterly. 'Richard probably thought you were making a play for him. And then to go on for half an hour about *Firing Line*—how obvious can you get?'

'But I *criticised* it,' said Morgan. 'I know he thinks he's God's gift to women, but surely even he can't be *that* arrogant.' He'd complained that she was *avoiding* him, for heaven's sake. 'And anyway,' she added with sudden conviction, 'I'm sure he wouldn't hold anything I did against you, Elaine.'

'And, of course, you know all about it,' said Elaine.

'Well, we were talking just now...' Morgan trailed off under Elaine's cynical gaze, which rested knowingly on her sister's long, bare thighs.

'I was just putting something in my room,' Morgan explained. 'I really don't think you have anything to worry about.'

Elaine looked sceptical. 'Morgan, Richard's about as straight as a corkscrew. He can sound fair-minded and impartial when it suits him, which is usually when he wants to get someone into bed. Bit of a Don Juan, our Richard.' She uncrossed her legs and looked complacently down at their smooth, graceful length. 'Which just means he hasn't met his match.' She gave Morgan a rather machiavellian smile. 'Yet.'

Morgan got under the covers without replying. She didn't doubt that Richard was not only ruthless but, in his own way, as devious as Elaine, and it was hardly news that he was used to bowling women over like ninepins, and probably not surprising if he had slept with a fair number of them.

If she'd been asked any time in the last three years, she'd have said he richly deserved his comeuppance. But, whatever Elaine said, she didn't believe that he tricked women into going to bed with him—why on earth should he when so many were willing without such tactics?

She was faintly surprised at how well she felt she knew him after such a short acquaintance. But before she could analyse this she remembered something that had puzzled her earlier.

'He said something rather odd earlier about getting his start exposing the Round Table. What was that all about?' she asked. At least it would keep Elaine from talking about whatever plans she was laying for Richard—something Morgan would, she discovered, very much rather not hear about.

'Oh, haven't you ever heard how he got started?' asked Elaine, pleased to show off her knowledge. 'It was just after he'd finished university. His mother had married some American millionaire and insisted Richard take up a job in one of the companies.

'Well, somehow he found out that old Hennessy's corporation had subsidiaries in the South, and that back in the early sixties, when Hennessy had been a senator for a northern state and very much on the side of the angels on civil rights issues, his company had been funding *anti*-desegregationist political campaigns, because they reckoned segregation kept labour costs down. Which might have been just ancient history if the company hadn't still had an absolutely lousy equal opportunities record twenty years down the line.'

Elaine digressed, intimidatingly, on an analysis of civil rights in American history and politics. There was no doubt about it—she was certainly a match for someone who had been acute enough even in his early twenties not just to uncover something embarrassing, but to recognise a political scandal when he saw one. Morgan fought down a stupid feeling of despondency and forced herself to pay attention.

'So next thing you know Richard published this detailed exposé, was on every chat show you can imagine, and, apart from pulling off a terrific scoop, absolutely wowed them all with the beauty and brains we know and love.'

Elaine stretched, then added offhandedly, 'I've always heard it was a disaster personally—it broke up the marriage, and his mother pretty much washed her hands of him—but it certainly made his fortune. Our esteemed chief practically went down on bended knees to get him onto *Round the Clock* along with Desmond, and after about a year they launched *Firing Line* and he's had it all to himself.' She gave another machiavellian smile. 'Until now.'

Morgan digested this in silence. 'What about his father?' she asked after a pause.

'Oh, he was a self-made man—construction, was it? Filthy rich, anyway, made a killing in the seventies when things were going up all over London.' Elaine crossed her legs again. 'Divorced her after seven or eight years, but there are no other children, so Richard should be getting quite a bundle one of these days,' she added complacently.

'How do you know these things?' asked Morgan with unwilling fascination.

'Morgan, darling, it's my business to know things; I'm a journalist, remember?' Elaine grinned. 'Comes in handy when I want to vet aspirants to my hand.'

Morgan stared at her. 'Has he actually—?'

'Not yet,' said Elaine, smiling again. She didn't say, But he will. She didn't need to.

CHAPTER FOUR

MORGAN spent an uneasy night. She felt as if she'd been playing chess with someone so much better that she couldn't even understand why she'd lost, as if even the rare intervals when the game had seemed to go her way had been strategic retreats which he'd somehow turned to his advantage.

Somehow she'd given information away even by the questions she *hadn't* answered—and Richard wasn't the kind of man to leave a secret unprobed. He would zero in on A Child's Place. . .and sooner or later he'd remember that he had a score to settle and that he had every reason to expose all its inefficiencies and half-successes to the cold light of day.

Morgan clutched her pillow and groaned, remembering that fateful Christmas party nearly a year and a half ago.

It probably hadn't been a bad party, but in Morgan's memory it looked more like a scene from hell—and not just because Elaine had had the bright idea of placing red Japanese lanterns over all the light fixtures. Probably someone had had a good time.

Morgan's memories began with her director, who'd cadged an invitation, making 'media contacts' and lapping up gossip about Richard Kavanagh—his ratings, his fame, his staggering postbag from female admirers. Then they leapt from this mildly embarrassing early stage to the hideously embarrassing events which had followed, beginning with the arrival of Richard Kavanagh himself, beautiful as Lucifer in the fierce white light of the hall, making his entrance unrepentantly and spectacularly late.

Half a dozen conversations had died down as everyone in the room had turned to the door as to a magnet. Every woman in the room had been staring at him—and even the men had been calling out jokes and questions, suspending their current conversations without a second thought.

And who could blame them? Morgan had been used by then to the contrast between the sister she'd grown up with and the jolly presenter of *Rise 'n' Shine*—somehow the performer was more sharply focused, more brightly coloured.

She'd supposed that it would be the same with Kavanagh—that the sizzling wit, the rather saturnine good looks would be muted to a fairly average sort of man in the flesh. But the fact was that the screen didn't do him justice: it blurred the strong but beautifully carved features, muddied the fine-grained skin, the pure brilliance of the quicksilver eyes, and above all gave no hint of the sheer physical energy of a body which seemed to have both the coiled strength and the faintly sinister grace of a whip.

It had been obvious that the party, which had been flagging, would now go on for as long as Richard Kavanagh chose to stay, and Morgan had dutifully started another round with a bottle and a plate of hors d'oeuvres. She'd come up to the newcomer's elbow in the middle of a rather caustic anecdote about one of his victims; an admiring crowd had gathered round, and he had been holding their attention effortlessly, but as he'd absently taken a glass from the tray Morgan had seen, with an odd shock, that the reverse was true. There had been a cynical boredom in the electrically charged eyes which had suggested that he would not be at this party for very long.

'Well, we got the bastards in the end,' he said with savage humour. Morgan felt an odd pricking of the nerves. Gazing unnoticed at that ruthless, handsome face, she felt as if she'd come up behind a panther and had suddenly realised the difference between watching it in the safe showcase of a nature programme and running the risk of actually attracting its attention. But he emptied his glass and held it out for a refill without bothering to look at her.

Then there was an interruption. A beautifully groomed woman in her late forties shouldered her way into the group.

'I don't believe we've been introduced,' she said. 'I'm Ruth Everett-Davies.'

'How do you do?'

While Morgan stood rooted to the floor, Ruth launched into a description of the organisation of which she was director, in the saccharine voice she always used when speaking of the charity to the public.

'If you'd seen, as I have, how much it means to a little girl who has, perhaps, nothing at home to call her own, no *home* of her own, for whom home may be nothing but a cardboard box in a subway, to have her own locker for her few, precious possessions. . . Pencils, paper, a ruler—things that you and I take for granted.' You would never have guessed, listening to her, that Ruth begrudged every issue of a pencil.

'I'm sure it's a very worthwhile cause.' He spoke in a drawling voice, slightly drunk, extremely bored. 'I'm afraid I've never heard of it, but if you'd like to send the details to my office. . .'

'I'll be happy to send you our literature, but we're all busy people; there simply isn't time to read everything that crosses one's desk. This won't take a moment,' Ruth said gamely.

'What exactly is it that you want me to do?'

Morgan would have given up in the face of that goaded exasperation, but Ruth was made of sterner stuff.

'We're holding a celebrity auction,' she said

promptly. 'You know, people bid to have Pavarotti sing "Happy Birthday" and so on.' *Pavarotti*?

'Yes?'

'We thought you might be willing to auction a kiss.'

'I see,' he said drily, while Morgan's toes seemed to curl inside her shoes. 'I hate to be a wet blanket, Ms. . .?'

'Everett-Davies.'

'But I think you're under a misapprehension about what I do. I'm not an actor, I'm a journalist—I like to think a good one. It's not part of my job to go into competition with professional sex symbols.'

'It would only take a few seconds of your time,' Ruth persevered.

'I'm afraid the answer is no.'

'It would mean so much to the children—poor, homeless little—'

But Morgan had had enough—enough of Kavanagh's superciliousness as well as Ruth's sycophancy.

'Really, Ruth, how could you expect one of the great political philosophers of our time to stoop so low?' she said sarcastically. 'Maybe you should auction off ten minutes of his views on GATT. I'm sure you could get a fiver for them.'

Kavanagh looked as startled as if one of his hors d'oeuvres had tried to bite him. 'Do I know you?' he asked. Morgan glowered at him.

'I don't see why *Firing Line* entitles you to be so high-minded all of a sudden,' she informed him. 'It's not even a fair fight—it *springs* things on people. Even a criminal gets to prepare his defence.'

'And the pillory went out a couple of hundred years ago,' he agreed, with a shrug. 'The answer is still no.'

'It's completely disingenuous to pretend your looks have nothing to do with *Firing Line*'s success,' Morgan continued superbly. She looked him up and down, managing to convey lofty superiority to people who

were susceptible to the looks in question—no easy
matter when a remote corner of her mind was simul-
taneously reaching the conclusion that he was, quite
simply, the best-looking man she had ever seen.

'You seem to kiss people all the time for your own
amusement,' she added crisply. 'I don't see why you
shouldn't do it for a good cause for a change. I'd do it
like a shot.'

There was a short, tense silence.

'*Would* you?' The same lazy, drawling voice didn't
sound quite so bored now.

Kavanagh took a step towards her. The light was
behind him; Morgan could see little more of his face
than a pair of satanic eyebrows and eyes bright with
daredevilry. He took the bottle of wine and the plate
of hors d'oeuvres from her hands and placed them
deliberately on the table beside him.

'Well, suppose you let me have one of yours and
we'll call ourselves quits?' he said softly. 'I'll give you
more than a fiver, anyway.'

Morgan took a step backwards. Kavanagh took
another step forward. Morgan stepped back again, and
again he stepped forward. His eyes, gleaming with
mockery, never left hers, and yet she knew, furiously,
that he was fully aware of the crowd now following his
every move, delighted by an unexpectedly amusing end
to a long party.

At last she came up against a wall and could go no
further. He propped himself against it with one arm,
looking down into her face, and for an interminable
moment nothing happened. It was obvious what was
going to happen; it was somehow the crowning humiliation that he would do this in full view of a roomful of
people—and why wasn't Ruth coming to her rescue?
He lifted her chin with one bent knuckle while the pad
of his thumb slid across her full lower lip, its slow
pressure parting her mouth. Morgan glared at him.

One bold black eyebrow swooped up in extravagant irony—he was enjoying himself *now* anyway. Well, Morgan had had enough.

She had, in fact, backed up, she discovered, to the door to a bedroom. She fumbled for the handle and pressed down, and to her relief the door swung in behind her. Surprise gave her a moment's advantage. She leapt backwards and, with a tomboy's instinctive physical co-ordination, sprang onto the bed, over a pile of coats, and flung up the window and swung over the edge to the narrow balcony outside while Kavanagh was still stumbling in the door and groping for the light.

The balcony ran the length of the flat, and at the far end was a fire-escape that she'd always had a hankering to try. Morgan was halfway to the head of the steps when a noise behind made her turn.

A pair of very long legs dangled from the window. Then, to her horror, a black figure propelled itself from the ledge down onto the balcony—and slipped. She heard him curse faintly as his feet slid along the icy cement and he struggled frantically to recover his balance. For one dreadful moment Morgan saw him teeter precariously over a railing five storeys up. And then he steadied himself and headed towards her.

Morgan gritted her teeth. In her mind's eye she suddenly saw with frightening vividness his hand reaching automatically for a second glass—and God only knew how many parties he'd been to already. He was obviously in no condition to take risks. She simply could not lead him on a dangerous chase down an icy fire-escape. Reluctantly she stood her ground, shivering in the wintry air.

It was a moonlit night, but the light was almost entirely blocked off by swags of holly, ivy and ever-green; Morgan could barely see him as he came inexorably on, a blacker shadow on the shadowy balcony. But every few paces he stepped briefly into a patch of moonlight, and the brilliant eyes glittered in the dark as if he really were the predator he'd reminded her of earlier.

'Now then, where were we?' said a sardonic voice in the dark.

By now Morgan was shivering from more than cold—but she wasn't about to let him see that. 'You were about to pay me five pounds and a penny to give Ruth a demonstration of your prowess,' she said acidly.

'And you decided such tender moments are best enjoyed in private. . .'

'I decided,' said Morgan in an even more acid tone, 'that it wasn't a fate worse than death, even if it was my fate and your death.'

He gave a crack of laughter, sounding genuinely amused. 'Do you realise you're being completely inconsistent?'

'I am *not*—'

'Of course you are.' In the faint glimmer of a streetlight far below she could see that he had thrust his hands into his pockets. 'You don't like the idea any better than I do when it comes right down to it.'

Morgan tried to slip by him, but he blocked her easily, his tall black figure moving only an inch or so on the narrow balcony.

'It's supposed to be a joke because it's just a kiss,' he continued coolly, as if nothing had happened. 'At least, I know the French use the word to cover a multitude of sins, but I take it my persecutor didn't mean me to take the lucky bidder to bed.'

'Of course not!' said Morgan. She was conscious of a strange feeling of unreality: here she was in the dark with her *bête noire*, while the relentless voice she knew from a hundred shows gave a logical dissection of a kiss.

'Of course not,' he agreed. 'No, it's just a kiss, and a kiss isn't real sex. We see actors doing it on screen all the time. But you're not an actress, and I'm not an actor, even if you can sometimes see my face on the box; I wouldn't know how to begin to pretend to kiss someone, and, like you, I don't much care for the idea of doing the real thing with someone I find unappealing, physically, morally or any other way—let alone doing it for an audience.'

He sounded perfectly serious; Morgan wondered cynically whether he believed a word of it. The fact was that his vanity had been injured; it wasn't a very flattering suggestion, and his ego had been dented. Now he was trying to turn that into some big moral principle.

'I hadn't realised you had such strong moral objections to the idea,' she said ironically. 'Of course there's no more to be said.'

It took a real effort not to betray her nervousness. In the course of his lucid little speech Morgan had made an unpleasant discovery: he was no more drunk than she was. The articulate, unhurried voice was emphatically not that of a man whose reflexes had been blunted by alcohol—which meant that, in a moment of misguided chivalry, she'd thrown away her advantage for nothing.

'You think I'm making a mountain out of a molehill?'

'Frankly, yes,' said Morgan.

'Because a kiss is just a kiss. Well, there's one way to find out.' And before she could back away again his arms closed around her, and he kissed her full on the mouth.

For a moment Morgan felt a queer, blind panic; she knew why she'd been running so desperately away from something which, on the face of it, represented nothing worse than a minor embarrassment. She felt as if she'd been forced up against something whose contact meant annihilation just as surely as if she'd been hurled down on the live rail of the underground. And then, after that first shock, she came to her senses—but to senses somehow amplified by that sizzling electric current.

She breathed in the mingled scents of male skin and damp wool and cigarette smoke. His cheek was rough, only hours from his next shave, and its roughness pricked her skin, but his mouth was as soft as velvet, tasting strongly of wine. Vaguely, in some remote corner of her mind, she supposed she saw his point— this was certainly nothing like the cinematic clinch that Ruth presumably had in mind. But why did he care, she wondered muzzily, if he was prepared to go through all this just to prove a point?

The moist tip of his tongue ran along the line of her half-parted lips. Morgan caught her breath. Perhaps his senses were heightened too, for at that almost imperceptible intake of air his arms tightened round her and he deepened his kiss. Incredulously Morgan found her knees actually going weak at this new assault on her senses; instinctively she clutched at him for support. And now, at last, he raised his head.

'Who are you?' he asked.

Morgan stared speechlessly up at him.

'What's your name?' he insisted, with a strange urgency.

And still Morgan was silent.

He looked down into her face, his eyes glinting beneath the devilish dark brows, and suddenly he smiled. 'You're right, it doesn't matter,' he said unforgivably, and added even more unforgivably, with the ghost of a laugh, 'My place or yours?' His mouth found hers again, and now his tongue took full possession of the mouth which had opened in protest.

And at this point, to her eternal embarrassment and dismay, Morgan lost her head. She took a sideways turn, drew her arm back, and landed a powerful right jab on his eye.

Even now, nearly a year and a half later, she cringed at the memory. It had been so uncool. So unsophisticated. So unfeminine. If she had to resort to crude violence, why not slap his face? And why resort to violence at all? Why not just say something bored and dismissive, like, 'That was quite nice, actually,' in a drawl as insulting as his own? Just about anything would have been better than punching him in the eye.

For the fifteenth time Morgan abandoned her attempts to sleep and buried her head in her pillow, trying to blot out the rest of this humiliating episode.

He had laughed softly and seized hold of her wrist. 'So I was right after all, was I?' he'd asked.

'Not at all,' Morgan had retorted, breathing fast. 'You weren't being asked for a French kiss, even in the English sense of the word.' She'd felt her fist strike home—what on earth would his make-up team make of it? Well, tough.

'Oh, it was my pleasure,' he said. 'My very great pleasure. You know, I could have sworn you were enjoying it; I don't usually go around forcing myself on unwilling women.'

Morgan ground her teeth. 'No, you usually get your kicks out of savaging people on the air, don't you?' she said coldly. 'Still, Christmas comes but once a year.'

He gave a short, unamused laugh. 'Is everyone from this charity so delightful?' he asked drily. 'No wonder you're hard up.'

'Now who's being inconsistent?' Morgan asked triumphantly.

He released her hand abruptly. 'I think I might be more impressed by this righteous indignation,' he remarked thoughtfully, 'if you hadn't waited for me to catch up.' The unlaboured irony was like the flick of a whip. 'If I were you,' he added softly, 'I'd think about whether I was so angry because I got something I didn't want. . .' an index finger traced, with casual contempt, her tingling mouth '. . .or because I got more than I bargained for.'

There was a short pause while Morgan tried to think of another withering repartee. At last he shrugged and walked back along the balcony to swing back up through the window into the flat. From outside, in the cold, sharp air, Morgan heard laughter and exclamations, and the voice of Richard Kavanagh, explaining ruefully that he'd walked into a door.

Morgan woke abruptly the next morning, heavy-eyed and apprehensive. Richard hadn't got a good look at her, of course. It had been a long time ago. But how long could she hope to get away with this? She imagined recognition dawning in his face, the sardonic, cynical gaze that would meet hers, and shivered involuntarily.

She slipped into the black jeans and sweatshirt that she normally wore on weekends—it didn't matter how she looked because Richard was *not* going to see her. . .

CHAPTER FIVE

'DON'T let him get away with that!' shouted Morgan.

'So wouldn't you agree—' continued Richard Kavanagh.

'No I would not,' said Morgan.

'—that consumers might not care to pay more for your recycled glass bottles if they knew their net energy cost was about the same as just making them from scratch? After all, sand isn't exactly a scarce commodity.'

'They *might* prefer not to turn the countryside into a landfill site,' said Morgan sarcastically. 'Other things being equal. But do you care? No.'

'People have to understand that these things take time. . .' said the hapless victim.

Morgan held her head in her hands and groaned.

It was half past eleven, at the end of a trying day. She had skulked in her room, waiting out breakfast, until the red car had disappeared down the driveway. Then she'd cleared every scrap of paper about the charity out of Richard's room, jumping every time a board creaked.

She'd spent most of the rest of the day cooped up in the house while it poured torrents outside, not because she minded the rain but because the house was the one place where she knew Richard was not. And at six o'clock she'd got tired of starting every time a door slammed and had announced that she was having dinner with Steve, ignoring the indignant protests and disappointed looks of her family.

Since Steve hadn't been expecting a visit from his old partner in crime, it wasn't really his fault that he

62

was out, but a two-hour wait in a chilly Land Rover
had done nothing to improve Morgan's temper. She'd
got home at last to find that everyone had already gone
to bed, and had retreated to the television for a dose of
her favourite spectator sport.

'So you're saying in this case there's no actual point
to recycling?'

'The *countryside* isn't exactly an unlimited commodity,' said Morgan, with a devastating imitation of the
Kavanagh drawl. 'As you know *perfectly* well, having
pulverised that councillor for encroachments on the
green belt just two months ago! This is complete
rubbish!' she shouted.

'Is that so?' said a familiar, sardonic voice from
behind her.

Morgan looked up in dismay.

'Care to argue with the real thing?' asked the real
thing, sinking down on the sofa beside her.

Morgan eyed him uneasily. 'I was just going to bed,'
she said.

'Rubbish.' There were drops of rain in his hair; he
must have just come in. He leant back against the sofa,
hands locked behind his head, long legs stretched out
in front of him. The grey eyes closed briefly, then
opened abruptly to stare at the screen. 'What's this
doing on at half past eleven on a Saturday—?' He
broke off at the sheepish look on Morgan's face. An
unholy grin lit up his own. 'Morgan, don't tell me
you—?'

'It's a subject that interests me,' she said. She
snatched up the remote control and turned off the
video. 'I'll watch this later; it's late,' she added
brusquely.

'For a non-fan you're pretty loyal,' he teased her,
still with that maddening smile lurking in his eyes.

Morgan looked at him suspiciously. The dark jeans
which strained over his muscular thighs, the pullover

which hugged his powerful chest made him look more like a rather thuggish cat burglar than a journalist, but he looked nothing like the monster who'd been haunting her imagination all day. Arrogant? Yes. Conceited? Undoubtedly. But she had to fight back the treacherous smile which threatened to break out in response to his.

She should go while the going was good—she felt as if he could actually see into her soul and see hundreds of ghastly, over-priced designer T-shirts stacked there. But his eyes seemed to dare her to stay, and Morgan found it almost impossible to refuse a dare...

'I hope you had a good day's digging,' she said innocently, just in case he'd forgotten that *everyone* didn't come when he called.

'Well, I could have done with a guide. Some of the places I need soil samples from are pretty unget-at-able.' A black eyebrow shot up mockingly. 'Too bad the Last of the Mohicans had other plans.'

The grey eyes narrowed as they focused on her face. 'I can't quite make you out...' The deep, drawling voice sent shivers up her spine. 'According to your family you're the quintessential tomboy—well, I suppose that's what you look tonight,' he admitted, taking in her black jeans and sweatshirt. 'But that wasn't exactly the picture you presented last night. I'd have thought all those exploits were something you'd put well behind you if it hadn't been for that damned tyre.'

Morgan recognised too late that intent, amused look. Oh, no, she thought, not *again*!

Don't run away, she told herself. Just sit quietly and make boring conversation until he loses interest. 'I—I don't think it's something you grow out of,' she stammered, her voice shaking with nervousness. She just had to keep talking until that dangerous look left his eyes. 'M-my mother never did.' What man wanted to hear about your mother? 'She was never afraid of anything, or anyone,' she said relentlessly. 'She lay down in front of a bulldozer when they started clearing ground for the factory—'

If anything, she saw nervously, the predatory gleam was more pronounced after this blatant red herring. 'And your parents divorced and lived happily ever after,' Richard said ruthlessly, showing in passing an unerring assessment of her rather conventional father. 'So last night *was* out of character.'

'I know I look ridiculous in make-up,' Morgan said edgily. There was no need for him to rub it in.

'What ever gave you that idea?' he asked, looking as much amused as astonished. 'I thought you looked pretty spectacular—you must have seen I couldn't take my eyes off you.'

For one fatal instant Morgan was distracted. Could it possibly be true? Was that why he'd been following her around? After Elaine's disparaging comments it was balm to her soul to imagine that someone with Richard's physical magnetism and *savoir-faire* could be attracted to her. And for a split second she let down her guard.

'Not that you need it.' The look in his eyes, resting on her bare face, made his meaning clear enough. He stretched out one hand unhurriedly, placing a single finger under her chin and tilting her face slightly to look at her more closely.

'It was lovely to look at,' he added judiciously. 'But I don't know any man who really likes a face covered in make-up.' His mouth quirked upwards. 'Personally I can think of few things less conducive to passion than a mouthful of grease.'

As if women had nothing better to think of than falling into his arms at the end of the evening! 'I always say a girl who goes out without freshening her lipstick is asking for it,' Morgan said tartly.

He gave a crack of laughter, his eyes sparkling with delight as she realised what she'd said. 'You're not

wearing any now,' he pointed out. The quicksilver eyes
held hers, inviting her to share his amusement. 'And I
was beginning to think you didn't fancy me,' he murmured, the infectious smile lighting his eyes.

Morgan felt her heart pounding in her chest. She
should put a stop to this. But his sheer physical
closeness seemed to affect her like a magnet—and for
one brief, heady moment it seemed as if he felt that
way too.

'But the question is. . .' he said softly, his mouth so
close that she could feel his breath, and paused.

'The question is. . .' he traced the line of her eyebrow
with a finger '. . .how did you look the last time we
met?'

Morgan came down to earth with a jolt. What an
idiot she'd been to think he could mean it! The whole
thing was a set-up. . .and she'd almost fallen for it!

'If this is one of your lines, Richard, I don't think
much of it,' she said caustically.

'Variation on a classic theme,' he murmured
unrepentantly.

Morgan jerked away from him abruptly and glared
at him. 'I thought you said the publicity gave people
the wrong idea, Richard,' she said acidly. 'As far as I
can see, your reputation doesn't begin to do you
justice.'

The electric grey eyes widened in astonishment at
the anger in her voice.

'I dressed to suit myself today because I didn't expect
to see you,' she went on dampingly. 'And the only
reason I dressed differently last night was because
Elaine said I should make an effort with my appearance—' She broke off in real dismay. Oh, if only she
hadn't got carried away by her longing to put him in
his place!

'Because someone from the studio was coming and
she wanted a shot at a job? What's so terrible about

that?' His amused voice allowed the moment of tension to slip away, leaving her feeling uncomfortably ungracious. 'Of course Elaine keeps her finger to the pulse— much use she'd be to me if she didn't.' He settled back unconcernedly against the sofa, long legs outstretched, his relaxed posture saying as clearly as any words that she'd overreacted.

Morgan stared at him, torn between suspicion and guilt at her *maladresse*. Was this another trap? It *sounded* reasonable enough. 'But—why on earth would you want a co-presenter?' she asked, with a feeling of burning her bridges. 'You invented *Firing Line*. Don't you hate the idea of sharing it?'

'Yes, in a way,' he agreed with a shrug. 'But it can't go on like this. The number of fans has snowballed over the last couple of years, and every time one of them pulls some crazy stunt it seems to attract more. So the ratings have gone through the roof, the Richard Kavanagh Admiration Society gets sillier by the minute, and meanwhile it's getting harder and harder to do the kind of investigation I like. A co-host, especially a woman, should help to defuse the hysteria.'

Morgan frowned. An unpleasant idea had occurred to her. Maybe he was right and she *had* been blinded by prejudice. At the moment he didn't sound a bit like the egotistical showman she'd despised. She'd taken it for granted that the attention was what he cared for, at least as much as the issues; it was staggering to find that the new post was actually his own idea.

Well, at least here was a chance to put in a good word for Elaine. 'I'm sure Elaine would be marvellous,' said Morgan. 'I know her style on *Rise 'n' Shine* is rather different—very flip and jolly, anything for a laugh. But that's what you need for breakfast TV, isn't it? You shouldn't underestimate her.'

'Oh, I don't underestimate Elaine; she's a professional to the core,' he said in a cool, indifferent tone.

'You're not much alike, are you? I can't imagine Elaine selling herself for less than her market value, let alone working for poor little homeless children at this place you still haven't told me about. . .'

There was a gleam of amusement in the grey eyes which Morgan was beginning to find all too familiar. There was no doubt about it, she admitted reluctantly—the spark of humour in that rather hard face was devastatingly attractive. But it was exasperating to see him once again effortlessly in control—and knowing it! However much his victims had at stake, for him it was never more than a game. Well, she'd see about that.

'I suppose it's hard for an only child to understand,' Morgan shot back. 'If someone's your sister you have a closeness which has nothing to do with how alike you are.' Well, it was almost true. She gave him a warm, sympathetic smile. 'You must have had a very lonely childhood.' It was a low blow, since it was probably true—but he was old enough now to look after himself.

To her surprise he laughed out loud. 'Not at all. It's sweet of you to be so sympathetic, but the fact is that I was sent off to boarding-school when I was eight and had an absolutely marvellous time.'

Morgan's eyes widened in dismay—this was worse than anything she'd imagined.

'No, don't look like that. I know it wouldn't suit lots of kids, but even then I was the same cocky bastard you know and loathe—I could do the lessons without much work, I was good at games and about as reckless as you are, which is saying something, and the net result was that I was king of the castle from day one.'

He grinned suddenly. 'My father was convinced that that sort of school would be a hotbed of vice, never having been to one himself, so he taught me a lot of dirty tricks to defend my virtue—and on the very first day I got in a fight with a boy three years older and won!'

Morgan laughed, unexpectedly disarmed. She had some idea of the tight spots that the man beside her had got himself into—and out of—over the years—and yet he still remembered this victory over an eleven-year-old Goliath. 'But didn't you miss your home?' she asked, her husky voice warm with a sympathy that this time was genuine.

'Home?' he asked blankly. 'Oh—well, I went to my mother in the holidays, but she was rather strapped for cash. My father gave her a hundred thousand pounds a year and swore he'd never give her another penny, and since her idea of economising was to buy from just one couturier...' He grinned reminiscently. 'He didn't mind sending extra money for me, though, so we used to spend hours dreaming up things I might need. I think my favourite idea was the lab—we thought science would appeal to an industrialist, so we said I wanted a fully equipped workshop to conduct chemical experiments.'

'Oh,' said Morgan. Not even to keep him off A Child's Place could she go on. Remembering what Elaine had told her, she found something unbearably poignant in his tone of affectionate amusement.

'Looking back, I suppose it was a bit hard on my father, but I reckoned he could afford it. It was all a game to me, so it somehow never occurred to me that my mother was serious about it.

'When I uncovered what Hennessy had been up to— Sorry, I'm just assuming you know all this.' He raised an enquiring eyebrow, his voice matter-of-fact.

Morgan nodded, vaguely ashamed of her briefing from Elaine the previous night. For the first time she had some idea of what it must be like to live in the full glare of publicity, with the most intimate details of your personal history a matter of simple public knowledge.

'I suppose I just took it for granted that she couldn't want to go on being married to someone like that. I'd no idea the money actually mattered.' He shrugged and laughed wryly. 'What a fool.'

'I'm sorry,' said Morgan helplessly.

'I was pretty melodramatic about it at the time.' His face, usually alive with mordant wit, was reflective. 'But she'd never had the slightest interest in politics, you know, and as far as she was concerned it had all been over and done with twenty years ago—so it must have looked like a combination of jealousy and sheer bloody-mindedness.'

He paused, then added more briskly, 'But in a way it was good for me to see that indifference to the issues—it made me see that you've got to *make* people care. And I suppose it gave me a sort of personal vendetta against the tinpot Napoleons of the world, which is no bad thing in my line of work.'

Morgan bit her lip. There was no trace of self-pity in his tone—if anything there was faint mockery of his younger self. But the note of amusement implied a cynical acceptance of flawed human relationships, the assumption that even those closest couldn't be trusted or relied on. The glimpse she'd had of the forging of that self-sufficiency chilled her.

'I'm sorry,' she said again, and impulsively put her hand on his arm. No sooner had she done it than she regretted it; she had no right to be offering comfort to someone who certainly hadn't asked for it. At best he would think her sentimental, at worst that she was making an advance while pretending not to. The problem was that it would look even worse if she instantly pulled her hand back. Reluctantly she met his eyes.

Well, looking on the bright side, he didn't seem to be sneering at her. He looked rather surprised, but gave her, she thought, quite a friendly smile. His eyes fell to her hand, and after a short pause he clasped it lightly in his; considering that she'd been completely out of line, this was a generous gesture, except that the slight pressure seemed to produce an electric shock in her palm which made it hard to go on looking merely friendly and matter-of-fact.

'Maybe I'd better have you instead of Elaine,' he remarked, flashing her a look gleaming with mischief.

'*What*?' said Morgan feebly.

'On the programme,' he explained. 'A few idle words and you've got me baring my soul to you—not something I do very often. Seems a shame to let all that talent go to waste. Or, come to think of it, maybe it's not such a good idea after all.' He paused, then added blandly, 'I think I function more effectively in one piece. Guerrillas I can cope with, but I don't want to go in fear of my co-host. What does your boyfriend do—wear a crash-helmet and a bulletproof vest?'

Morgan suppressed a sigh. The master of *Firing Line* was off and running. Back to his old tricks. She gave him a challenging look. 'Is that a roundabout way of asking whether I have a boyfriend?' she asked.

'Yes,' he said instantly.

'Do you have a girlfriend?' she asked pertly. 'Or are we talking double figures?'

'It's usually one at a time,' he said. 'My affairs tend to be intense but short-lived.' Of course a girlfriend *would* mean an affair with him. 'And no, I'm not seeing anyone just now.' His eyes held hers challengingly. 'You haven't answered me,' he reminded her. 'Are you seeing anyone? Or is all your time given up to this mysterious job of yours?'

Morgan met his eyes uneasily. Just because he'd had a difficult childhood it didn't mean he wasn't a dangerous opponent—and that brief moment of sympathy made him more, not less dangerous. Hadn't she seen him set up this trap on *Firing Line* time after time, forcing the victim to choose between two things he didn't want to talk about, pinpointing the real weak spot—the subject the victim avoided at all costs...? And for all his superficial good humour there was an unyielding set to his mouth which did not bode well for her chances of fobbing him off for much longer.

'If you won't tell me about your job,' Richard went on nonchalantly, 'the least you can do is tell me about your love life.' His eyes mocked her. 'So how about it? Have you always expected it to be for ever and a day, or have your lovers been people you lusted after and forgot?'

He dealt her another of those dazzling, knee-weakening smiles, but the brutal phrasing was like a slap on the face. Get too close to me at your peril, it said. But Morgan never refused a dare.

She looked Richard straight in the eye.

'Is that what you do?' she asked. 'Play the field?' She would beat the master interviewer at his own game if it *killed* her. And for a moment she thought she had him on the run.

'You never give up, do you?' he asked exasperatedly.

'That's not an answer.'

'All right, then, since you find the subject so fascinating...' He scowled at her. 'I suppose you could say they were like stories—you can be passionately involved in one without expecting it to be your life's work.'

'This week's news is next week's history...'

A black eyebrow quirked upwards suddenly, as if he was amused by her inevitable disapproval. 'If one's honest one admits it has something to do with the thrill of the chase.' He shrugged. 'Anyway, when I'm working I can't think about anything else—I tend to get swallowed up in a story, and when I surface again I'm mildly surprised to see that some girl I'd been seeing isn't around any more.'

'You're not interested in love, is that it?' Morgan asked ruthlessly.

The electric eyes widened in astonishment. Morgan tensed for the inevitable snub.

'It's not exactly up to me, is it?' he said at last, with another shrug. 'If someone plays the pools and wins a hundred pounds, you don't say, But wouldn't you rather have a million? They can't hand back what they've won and say they'd rather have the jackpot.' His eyes mocked her. 'It might be nicer to buy a tropical island and live in paradise for the rest of your life—but if a weekend in Brighton is all you can afford you might as well enjoy it and not worry because you can't stay longer.'

'Oh,' said Morgan. For the second time that evening she felt uncomfortably as if she had been seeing him through a veil of prejudice.

'And now,' said Richard pleasantly, 'it's your turn.'

Morgan tried desperately to think of something to say that would not sound pathetic. 'Oh, most of my friends have been boys—men,' she said reluctantly. 'And of course I've gone out with people.'

'But you're not interested in sex,' he completed blandly.

Morgan gritted her teeth. 'Just because you like someone a lot doesn't mean you think of them that way. . .' she floundered, wishing that she could sink into the ground. This was the kind of thing you could tell a woman friend if you had one; it was the kind of thing you told a sister if you were close. It was *not* the kind of thing you confided to a man who tossed aside the woman of the week with the Sunday supplements.

'But every so often someone gets the wrong idea,' he remarked shrewdly.

'Well, you should know all about that,' Morgan said waspishly. You needn't think I think about you that way, she added silently.

'I'm beginning to,' he said wryly.

Morgan had thrust her hands in her pockets in a defiant, defensive posture that was anything but provocative, and the ancient five-a-side Sunday football sweatshirt left everything to the imagination. But suddenly, under Richard's cynical gaze, she had an uncomfortable glimpse of another view of herself.

'You get to be friends through rock-climbing or whatever, and you think you're just one of the lads. . .' he went on mockingly, as if the sweatshirt, slopping over the decidedly unboyish curve of hips hugged by tight black jeans, had been perversely designed to set the male imagination working overtime. 'But then suddenly you find he's reading much more into it than just friendship. . .'

Morgan stared at him. The clever, magnetic face seemed to know all about incidents which had less to do with sex than with ridiculous misunderstandings—embarrassing episodes which someone so glamorous couldn't possibly know by personal experience, but which he seemed to understand anyway.

He raised an eyebrow. 'Poor devils,' he added, shaking his head. 'They think you're leaving all that make-up off to lead them on.'

'I'm sure it seems ridiculous to you,' Morgan said edgily.

'Not at all. They have my sympathy.'

'What about me?' she demanded indignantly.

There was a short silence. The brilliant grey eyes scanned her face. 'I think,' he said at last, with a rather odd note in his voice, 'that you can probably look after yourself.'

CHAPTER SIX

DAMN Richard!

Morgan scowled at her reflection in the mirror. She was dressed for church in her long, loose dress of many-layered white gauze, and if it hadn't been for Richard she would have been downstairs eating her breakfast twenty minutes ago. Instead she'd spent twenty minutes trying to decide whether to do something about her face.

For the tenth time she concluded irritably that whether she put make-up on or left it off it would look as though it was for his benefit. Damn him! She could just imagine the mockery in his eyes as he glanced to her mouth to see whether she was wearing lipstick.

She lingered a moment longer until she realised in exasperation that she was trying to see the fragile-looking creature in the glass through Richard's eyes. Who cares what he thinks? she thought crossly. She put lipstick on her mouth and wiped it off again.

All this agonising made her late. When she got downstairs her parents had already gone to church with the children, leaving a note on the kitchen table instructing Morgan to come with Elaine. Elaine was nowhere to be seen. Neither was Richard.

Perhaps Elaine was starting up the car? Morgan walked out the back door and around the side of the house and stopped dead in her tracks. Elaine stood beside a familiar, mud-bespattered red sports car, hands propped on the window-frame, head and shoulders inside. It was only too obvious what was going on. Well, it was nothing to her; *she* certainly didn't want to

be the next on Richard's hit list. Morgan was about to
turn hastily away when Elaine stood back from the car.

'Oh, here's Morgan now,' she said unembarrassedly.
Her blonde hair gleamed in the sun; her shift of stone-
washed pink silk was devastatingly sophisticated in its
simplicity.

'We'd better get going,' Morgan said curtly, not
looking at the red car.

'Right you are,' said Elaine cheerily. 'Look, why
don't you take my car? Richard and I have a couple of
things to discuss.'

She tossed the keys over. Morgan fielded the haphaz-
ard throw automatically and stalked to her sister's car,
ignoring the mocking 'Well held' which emerged from
the depths of the sports car. A few things to discuss?
Ha!

Presumably because they had so much to 'discuss',
Elaine and Richard had fallen well behind by the time
Morgan drew up in front of the village church. She
went inside to join the family in a pew near the front;
it was a good ten minutes before Elaine slid into the
pew beside her. And it was only after another quarter
of an hour, during which Morgan had kept her eyes
fixed firmly forward or down at her prayerbook, that
she glanced out of the corner of her eye and realised
that Richard hadn't come in as well.

Morgan managed, after a fashion, to follow the rest
of the service; she managed to shake hands and chat
with people afterwards, giving Elaine a chance to
volunteer information. But when they met at Elaine's
car, with the red sports car parked immediately behind
it, and still Elaine said nothing, curiosity got the better
of her.

'Where's Richard?' Morgan asked casually.

Discretion warred with Elaine's longing to show off.
'They've a skeleton staff at Triple Q on Easter Sunday,'
she explained knowledgeably. 'Apparently he's sweet-

talked a couple of the workers into smuggling him in to have a look around.'

'Well, I suppose if anyone could it would be Richard,' Morgan said doubtfully. In the past the workers had shown a grim solidarity against everyone hostile to the plant.

'Very hush-hush, of course. They're having him come round the back—he took the path behind the car park here.'

Morgan frowned. A vague feeling of uneasiness gnawed at her. 'I wonder why they didn't have him take the path from the head of the canal? This one's been a dead end ever since they abandoned work on the bypass—Nick and Steve and I used to play at the far end when we were—' When we wanted to ambush each other.

She stared with dawning apprehension at her sister. Elaine hadn't liked the rough games that had appealed to Morgan and her friends; it wouldn't have occurred to her that this was an impossible route into the plant. But Morgan knew the terrain around Triple Q as well as her own family farm—the fact that it was out of bounds had only given playing there an added spice.

She frowned into space, her heart cold; in her mind's eye she saw the long, rocky path tracing its way up a narrow ravine blocked with rubble, the steep slopes to either side offering perfect concealment for enemies.

She could see all too easily the anger Richard could have aroused in men who saw their jobs at risk—*put* at risk by someone whose own career would get a boost from the scandal, someone whose tabloid notoriety would have made him instantly recognisable as the spoilt darling of fortune. He was almost certainly walking into a trap. . .

'We've got to stop him,' she said abruptly.

'*What*?'

Morgan sketched in the position, the words tumbling

over themselves in her anxiety. 'I can catch up if I go by water, but I'll need your car, Elaine,' she concluded.

To her astonishment a faint smile curved her sister's lovely mouth. 'You like him, don't you?' asked Elaine.

'*Like* him?' Morgan exclaimed. 'He's the most arrogant man I've ever met! But obviously if he needs help—'

The smile broadened, but Elaine shook her head. 'Richard can look after himself, Morgan. He's been working on this for months—he wouldn't thank you for sticking an oar in. I think we'd better just go back to the house.'

The note of finality in her voice made it plain enough that further argument would be useless.

Morgan looked wildly round the car park at the clusters of flowery frocks and summer suits. Her father wouldn't let her take the Land Rover and leave the family stranded—not without good reason, anyway. And if he knew what she had in mind he'd do his best to stop her. So *how*. . .?

She was on the brink of outright panic when she realised, with a wild rush of relief, that help was at hand. Her old friend Steve, almost unrecognisable in suit and tie, was standing by a rather battered Mini.

Five minutes later the Mini was toiling up the old canal road. Over the complaints of the engine came fragments of a diatribe from the harassed driver. 'Out of your mind. . .bloody insane. . .never change. . .time you grew up. . .' he expostulated, ending only as they pulled up by the boathouse where the canal met the river.

His fair round face flushed with effort, Steve helped Morgan to haul a boat and oars to the bank, then stared, appalled, at the river.

'You're not getting me on that again,' he said emphatically.

Morgan looked down uneasily. As a child she'd always been strictly forbidden to take boats on the river, even though the really dangerous falls were far away in town, and she'd defied this only once, in an ill-fated if exhilarating expedition down a minor set of rapids in a punt. Steve had *dared* her to do it. Well, that had obviously been foolhardy, but she had an uncomfortable feeling that taking a rowing-boat out was not much better.

A rainy week had left the river high and full; the sleek brown water raced away from the weir as if anxious to throw itself over the cataracts well ahead. But its speed would stand in her favour. Richard would take over an hour to reach the obstruction in his path. She might easily be there in twenty minutes. And they would be miles above the danger zone, after all, she reminded herself. There was no *question* of taking the boat into the white water close to town. It was simply a matter of collecting Richard and rowing across the river to safety.

'Don't be silly,' she said firmly. 'It can't go wrong. And anyway, I've got to *rescue* someone.'

'Well, sooner him than me,' remarked her faithless childhood companion, but he helped her attach the painter to a ring and lower the boat to the water. He watched sceptically as Morgan kicked aside her long skirt and leapt agilely into the boat.

'Sure you want to go ahead with this?'

'What do you think?' asked Morgan.

Steve hesitated, looking more like an office-bound junior accountant than the fearless boy she'd once known. But at last he shrugged and untied the moor-ing—and the boat was borne swiftly away downstream.

For the next quarter of an hour all was well. Morgan had to sit facing forward to keep an eye out for the rendezvous, but with a little practice she became fairly adept at handling the oars in this position. The banks swept by, and at last she saw the file of pylons rising above a mound of rubble—and a couple of figures silhouetted against the sky. The end of the path should be just the other side of this flank of the hill.

Morgan began pulling for the right bank. But now, for the first time, she realised the full strength of the current—before she'd drawn more than a few feet towards the bank she'd been snatched another ten yards downstream. She glanced desperately up the hillside. Yes, there was Richard now, but she was nearly level with him already—in a couple of minutes she would be out of sight.

'Richard!' she shouted. '*Richard*!' Had he heard her? '*Help*!' she screamed, struggling to steer the boat to shore. '*He-e-e-e-lp*!'

Out of the corner of her eye she could see Richard coming downhill, bounding over the rocky ground in a way that would have terrified her if she had not been involved in a struggle for her own survival. He stumbled once, recovered, and then he was pelting down the bank.

He reached the wet rocks just ahead of her.

In the split second as the boat went by he managed to grab its rope. Bracing his feet in the rocks, he began to draw the rope back, hand over hand, against the full weight of the current.

Behind him Morgan saw nine or ten men begin to descend the hillside. She called out a warning, and as Richard glanced instinctively back over his shoulder his feet slipped on the wet rocks and he was pulled into the water behind her.

The boat rocketed headlong downstream while Morgan struggled to steer now for the opposite bank, Richard dragged behind by the rope. She was still fighting desperately to bring the boat under control when they hit white water half a mile further down.

She winced as the boat bucketed over a line of jagged rocks. Why didn't he let go?

He must be caught in the rope, she realised with a spurt of fear.

Suddenly she felt the boat pulled up short as he wedged his feet between two rocks. 'Get out!' he shouted over the roaring water. 'You can climb over the rocks here!'

A rock broke free; the precarious foothold was lost, and they jolted forward. But now they went by jerks and starts as he dug his feet in again and again, battling against the current. 'Jump, damn you!' he shouted.

Morgan hesitated. The falls were only a mile away; if he slipped again after she jumped, she would have no control over the boat and could do nothing to help him. And even as the doubt presented itself the water swept him from his last foothold and snatched the boat inexorably forward.

Morgan gritted her teeth. There was a railway bridge just before the falls; if she could wedge an oar in its supports, it would give Richard a chance to climb free.

Ignoring the shouts from behind, she continued to pull as best she could for the left bank. And when the bridge was only a few yards away she dropped her right oar and took the left oar in both hands, and as they came to the first support she thrust the oar into the angle between two metal struts and held on with all her might.

The force of the water drove the oar painfully into her ribs, but she held on. And now, thank God, Richard was climbing out of the water. He was holding the iron support with one hand, the rope with the other. . .

Hadn't he been trapped after all?

The oar tilted and slid, and the boat shot forward, snatching the rope from his hand.

'For God's sake *jump*!' he shouted. And at last Morgan sprang from the boat.

Her foot skidded backwards, and she almost missed the support she'd aimed for, her hands scrabbling desperately at the slimy metal. Then, just as she had found a purchase she was almost wrenched away again. The long, wet tail of her skirt had caught on a rowlock and now held her firmly tied to the boat, which was straining to hurl itself down the current.

Morgan kicked back, trying to dislodge the wet, twisted fabric. The problem was that she couldn't spare a hand to pull it free. If she could only stand up she might be able to free a hand, she thought, but as she pulled herself painfully up the boat plunged abruptly sideways, smashing her cruelly against the piling. She cried out and lost her footing, and slid back into the water.

Her hands were tired from clutching the oars. She could feel her grip weakening. And then, just as she thought she could hold on no longer, a dark shape appeared, silhouetted against the light. In an instant Richard was at her side.

He took in the situation at a glance. With a single, swift movement he grasped the twisted skirt and tore it ruthlessly off, then tossed it away. Morgan saw the boat speed past, launch off into space where the water fell away, and then disappear.

Richard took hold of her wrists and pulled her ungently to her feet. 'You bloody fool!' he said savagely.

Morgan flinched. 'We can wade ashore from here,' she said quietly. 'It's only really deep in the centre — it's that deep, narrow channel that makes the water so fast.' She clambered through the supports and began wading through waist-high water to the bank. Richard followed her, the angry voice lashing her like a whip.

'What kind of crazy, crack-brained stunt was this supposed to be? And why the *hell* didn't you get out when I told you? You could have been killed.'

'Don't be ridiculous,' said Morgan wearily. She sat down abruptly in the shallow water at the river's edge, too tired to move further. 'Are you all right?' she asked, looking up at him. His face was cut and bruised and unusually pale; he looked as if he'd been through a fight.

'Oh, I'm all right,' he said. He sat down beside her. 'How about you?'

'Oh, I'm fine,' said Morgan.

'Good,' said Richard. 'Then I can do this.' He pulled her into his arms and kissed her ruthlessly on the mouth.

A very long time later he raised his head for breath. 'I've been wanting to do that ever since I first saw you,' he remarked with satisfaction. And did it again.

Morgan knew better than to make too much of this—he was obviously suffering from reaction. In fact, she was probably suffering from reaction herself. That would explain why his kiss had such a peculiar effect on her. She'd kissed boys before, but it had never felt like a slug of brandy.

A much longer time later he raised his head again, and pushed her wet hair back from her face.

Morgan looked him straight in the eye. Her earlier exhaustion had vanished as if by magic—which meant that she was no longer too tired to give as good as she got. At least this time she could do better than 'How dare you?'

'But Richard,' she said reproachfully, 'you said if I tried any more silly stunts to get your attention you'd give me something to remember you by that I wouldn't like.' She paused, with the instinct for timing that she'd picked up from a master of the game. And then, after he'd waited a few seconds for her to go on, 'But that was *wonderful*,' she said guilelessly. 'But I wasn't trying to get your attention. *Really*, I wasn't.'

For just a split second she thought she'd caught him

off guard at last—but he threw his head back and gave
a shout of laughter. 'You must be all right,' he said. 'I
was beginning to be worried.' He gave her a devilish
grin. 'But I'm sorry it wasn't any good for you, darling.
I'll see if I can't do better this time—third time lucky.'
And he kissed her again.

Much, much later he drew his head away, his mouth
parting from hers reluctantly. His eyes seemed to
devour her—it was as if his only reason to stop kissing
her was to look at her again.

'That's quite a pick-me-up,' admitted Morgan.

'Then kiss me back,' he said very softly.

Morgan's eyes fell to his moist, supple mouth. She
swallowed hard. There were all kinds of reasons why
this was a very bad idea.

'Elaine *said* you wanted to go to bed with me,' she
said, with a shaky smile.

'I'd have thought you could have worked that one
out for yourself,' he said instantly, not missing a beat.

Morgan stared at him.

'Was I supposed to simper coyly and pretend the
thought never crossed my mind?' he asked impatiently.
His face was still white, but the old fighting spirit was
obviously raring to go. 'Another thing I've been wanting to do ever since I first saw you, though this is hardly
the place to make up for lost time.'

'Are you sure you're all right?' asked Morgan. 'Did
you hit your head? Are you sure you're not thinking of
Elaine?'

'Of Elaine?' he said blankly.

'She's so—well—sexy,' said Morgan, thinking of
Elaine's microscopic skirts, gleaming legs and high
heels. Morgan always tripped over high heels, laddered
tights, and worried about how to dispose her legs in a
short skirt; she knew she'd never manage that sleek,
delectable look in a million years.

He raised one bold, sceptical eyebrow—it was odd

to see that typical Kavanagh expression on a muddy, bloodstained face. 'Are you serious? My God, you *are* serious. Morgan, darling, Elaine's a very attractive girl, but she doesn't send my blood pressure rocketing through the roof the way you do—and not just because you always seem to be half-dressed or soaked to the skin. It's not just the way you look—you've got a voice that makes "pass the salt" sound like the kind of thing we can't say on the air before nine p.m.'

His eyes narrowed, as if he was trying to bring her into sharper focus. 'And then, I don't know, I wouldn't have said you were very sexually experienced, but you have this wild, crazy courage, this complete lack of other physical inhibitions that's rare in adults—I'd love to know. . .' His voice trailed off, but the frank assessment in his eyes was as clear as any words.

Morgan stiffened and tried to pull away from him; she felt as if she'd been suddenly brought up clean, cold sober from the intoxication of his kisses.

His arm tightened around her, holding her against him in the shallow, muddy water. 'Sorry, have I offended you?' he asked.

'No, but it seems very cold-blooded. Do you talk this way to everyone you want to sleep with?' she asked. Suddenly she felt wet and bruised and cold.

'I wouldn't usually be such a fool,' he said cynically. 'It must be having such a close shave, or perhaps— The other thing I was going to say was that your eyes have this rather terrifying, terrible honesty—even when you're trying desperately to be diplomatic *they* always say exactly what you're thinking! They seem to dare one to match that; to lower one's defences and say what one thinks.' He smiled at her. 'They're doing it now, you know. They seem to say you'd rather have the truth than whatever I might think you'd like to hear.'

Morgan shifted slightly and then winced as she jarred

her leg. They both looked down to find blood staining the water.

'Morgan—*are* you all right?' he asked. 'This looks bad. Can you stand up?'

She struggled to her feet, and they could now see the long gash along her left thigh. Richard gave a low whistle.

'It's just a scratch,' said Morgan. 'But I suppose I should disinfect it; this water isn't very clean. Didn't you say you had a first-aid kit in the car?'

'Which is a good ten miles cross-country from here, by my reckoning. . .'

Morgan began to laugh helplessly. 'Oh, Richard, I thought you knew,' she said. 'We're back where you started. The car park is just at the top of the bank.'

He stared at her speechlessly for a moment. 'Can you walk?' he said at last.

'Yes,' Morgan said grimly, taking a painful step.

'No,' said Richard. Without pursuing the discussion he scooped her up into his arms and began striding up the bank.

Morgan glared at him. 'I expect you were the kind of Boy Scout who bullied old ladies into crossing roads,' she said sourly. 'And then picked their pockets when they weren't looking.'

'Sure,' said Richard. 'But I always gave half the money to charity—just like all the really big crooks— sorry, shrewd businessmen. That was the *next* day's good deed.'

Morgan choked back a laugh. In spite of herself she was startled by the iron strength of the arms which held her. It was with genuine curiosity that she said, after a minute or so, 'I thought journalism developed your intellectual muscles. What do you do—work out with a punching bag in case you can't batter someone with questions?'

He raised an eyebrow. 'Everyone doesn't play by the

rules, Morgan.' He picked his way round a row of
bottle banks and added, 'I'm sure you'll be glad to hear
that I don't have things entirely all my way. No one's
ever actually acted on the death threats, but I have had
hired thugs set on me to—what shall I say?—wreak a
little limited damage. If it comes to that, I like to be
able to put up a fight—though, of course, if they send
enough people there's a limit to what you can do.'

Now was the time to explain, Morgan thought muzzily, but her leg was throbbing and it was hard to think
straight. By the time she had begun to put a sentence
together Richard had set her down by the car and was
kneeling to find the spare key under the chassis, having
lost his in the river. Shivering, she began to peel off her
ravaged tights while he took the first-aid kit from the
boot.

Out of the water she was suddenly conscious of being
distinctly underdressed. No matter which way you
looked at it, one pair of cotton briefs and one drenched
bodice with a few shreds of skirt were scant protection
either against the spring air or against someone who'd
just been telling her about after the effect this sort of
thing had on the male imagination.

But Richard seemed, for the moment, to have set
that train of thought aside. He dropped to one knee
beside her and put antiseptic paste on a wad of cotton
wool in a businesslike way. 'I'm afraid this will hurt,'
he apologised, 'but I'll try to be quick.' He began to
dab gently at the wound.

'That's enough, you sadist; give the white blood cells
something to do for a change,' Morgan said after a
pause.

He screwed the top back on the tube. 'All right.' He
looked up at her with a glint in his eye. 'And now it's
your turn. You practically sent me to Siberia just now
for admitting to something so crass as curiosity. What

about you? Don't you wonder what it would be like?
The truth now.'

Morgan stared into his eyes. She knew what his
kisses were like now; what would he be like as a lover?
If she was honest, she did wonder. And at the thought
of admitting it she realised that there was an erotic
charge in baring one's soul, too; just the thought of
saying the word 'yes' sent a chill down her spine.

'Possibly,' she temporised.

He gave a shout of laughter. '*Possibly*?'

'Yes, then,' Morgan admitted, her grey eyes
troubled. 'But what about Elaine?'

'Oh, she must have gone back to the house by now.'
He grinned. 'Shame we can't satisfy our mutual curiosity just now, but why don't you sit on my lap and kiss
me again?' He opened the car door with a flourish. 'I
wouldn't want you to catch cold.'

Morgan shook her head.

He sank into the seat and took her hand. 'Why not?'
he asked. 'I'm not saying that what your body wants is
necessarily what you want—a million starving dieters
can't all be wrong. But don't you think you owe it
something pretty substantial by way of compensation?'

Morgan smiled reluctantly. 'But what about Elaine?'
she repeated.

'What *about* Elaine?' he said impatiently. 'She's
talented and hard-working, and if it makes you any
happier she gets my vote—though they won't appoint
someone just on my say-so. I think she'll be a first-rate
colleague, and I hope she joins me on the show. I
wasn't planning to marry her.'

'If that's a proposal, the answer is no,' said Morgan,
but she allowed him to take her hands and draw her
down into his lap.

'Have a heart; I haven't even got round to the
proposition yet,' he murmured, brushing her lips
with his.

'The answer is still no,' said Morgan.

His arms tightened around her. 'You're impossible. But I'm glad you're in one piece—even if you have thrown a spanner into something I've been working on for months.' He drew his head back, smiling slightly. 'What on earth possessed you to take a boat onto that kind of water? What was this supposed to be—the Lady of Shalott going over Niagara?'

'I came to rescue you, Richard,' said Morgan.

Her heart seemed to stop as his smile slowly faded. 'You what?' he asked softly.

'Elaine t-told me about the path you were taking,' she stammered. 'The thing is, Richard, it couldn't possibly be legitimate; there's *zillions* of easy, quicker secret ways into Triple Q, whereas that path has been a dead end for *years*. I mean—don't you see?—the workers there *hate* people trying to undermine the place because they've had to go through such hell taking the jobs in the first place, so I was afraid it was a trap. So I just took the quickest way I could to get there. . .' Her voice trailed off under the rigidly controlled fury in the steel-grey eyes.

'I see,' he said. 'You'd no idea what I was working on, or who I was working with, but you felt you naturally had a better idea of whether they were to be trusted. I've always thought feminine intuition would come in handy; actual research can be so tiresome.'

Morgan swallowed. 'I'm sorry,' she said. 'But I was afraid they'd beat you up.'

There was a short silence. He met her eyes unsmilingly, taking in the bedraggled hair, the torn dress, the earnest expression. His face, bruised and battered, with a gash on one temple, looked for a moment frighteningly grim; his mouth was clenched shut, as if he was afraid of what he might say if he opened it. But then, incredibly, one corner twitched.

'You were afraid they'd beat me up,' he said. 'Not kill me?'

'I don't *think* they'd kill you,' she said.

'Just rough me up a bit, is that it?' The faint smile spread wider.

'I didn't want you to get hurt,' she explained.

For a moment she seemed to have taken his breath away. Then, abruptly, he gave a shout of laughter. His split lip began to bleed again; at her look of concern he began laughing helplessly.

'I'm so glad you come along,' he managed to say. He burst out laughing again and winced. '*Damn.*' The cold grimness had gone; an exasperated tenderness had taken its place. 'Well, it was marvellous of you to go to so much trouble, Morgan, but, if I could just ask a favour, don't go rescuing me again until I've recovered from this time.'

Morgan suppressed a sigh. It was all very well for him to joke about it; if he'd consulted her in the first place none of this would have happened. Now he'd gone back to thinking her completely ridiculous. It was better than that cold, steely look, but still. . .

'We'd better get back to the house to change.'

'Into what? one asks oneself,' he remarked. 'I rather think my suitcase holds nothing but insoluble problems for laundries. The rate of attrition on my wardrobe this weekend has been pretty spectacular.' He shot Morgan a mocking glance. 'But perhaps memory deceives.'

Morgan smiled feebly.

'Anyway, now that I realise you were saving my life I really think the least I can do is a programme on your charity.' He grinned. 'Maybe I'll find out just what it is you do for a living.'

'You saved *my* life,' Morgan said hastily. 'You don't owe me anything. And I really don't think you'd be interested.'

Richard raised an eyebrow in surprise. 'Maybe not,

but I don't mind having a look. . .' He gave her a friendly smile.

'I think you'd be wasting your time,' she said desperately.

'I'll have a word with the director when I get back to London. Who is it runs the place?'

'Ruth Everett-Davies,' Morgan said, giving up the fight. She stole a glance at Richard. Her heart sank. He'd been looking tired, and slightly perplexed by her resistance to something that she must know could do the charity a lot of good. Now his eyes were grim.

'Everett-Davies?' he said. 'I rather think I know her already. . . She was at one of Elaine's parties a couple of Christmases ago, wasn't she?'

'She might have been,' Morgan murmured.

His eyes looked at her thoughtfully. Their chilly distaste seemed to go through her like cold steel. Now, at last, at the worst possible moment, Richard Kavanagh had remembered what she'd done the first time they'd met.

'It was you, wasn't it?' he asked.

'Yes,' admitted Morgan almost inaudibly. 'It was me.'

CHAPTER SEVEN

A LOW hum filled the classroom, where some forty-five
children, in groups of six and seven, were gathered
around large, scratched Formica tables. In the far
corner, Morgan manhandled a roll of newsprint to the
ground.

Now eager hands helped her to unroll it. The children had never seen such a long piece of paper; the
new project—a geographical mural that would go right
around the classroom—began to look like fun. It was
obvious that they could hardly wait to start in on the
sheet with paint and felt-tip pens; Morgan just hoped
that she could scrounge enough implements to paint in
the vast surface.

She was backing her way to the door when it opened,
and she heard Ruth's voice behind her.

'And this is one of our classrooms.' Ruth gave a little
laugh. 'Well, I see everyone is busy! I'll just show you
a *couple* of things, and then introduce you.'

Morgan took this as a hint that Ruth wanted her
visitor to herself for a bit longer, and continued backing
along the aisle.

'Most of these were made by the children themselves,' Ruth continued, from across the classroom.
'We feel this gives them a real *pride* in the place, a
sense of *belonging*. Look at this, for instance—
"Languages of the Classroom". Every time a child joins
the class who comes from a background not represented, he or she is invited to add to the table—you
see, a few simple words in each language. We feel it's
so important to be *genuinely* multicultural. . .'

The classroom had fallen perfectly silent. The children didn't like Ruth, who talked about them as if they weren't there, and could never remember anyone's name; and though Morgan had never talked about it they'd somehow worked out why the classroom was always recycling its supplies. In the silence the footsteps of the newcomers sounded unnaturally loud.

Morgan straightened up at last and turned to greet the guest.

Beside Ruth stood a tall, black-browed, sardonic man in a dark suit and yellow tie. The last time Morgan had seen him his face had been bruised and bloody and smeared with mud, and his eyes had seared her with contempt. Now he was formidably point-device—she remembered abruptly that she already bore the spills of chalk and smears of paint which teaching always seemed to entail—and his face wore an expression of bland courtesy.

'And this is Morgan Roberts, one of our *wonderfully* dedicated staff,' enthused Ruth. 'You probably know her sister, Elaine, from *Rise 'n' Shine*—so talented.'

They had drawn near Morgan. 'We've met,' he said, and shook her hand briefly.

'*Marvellous*,' cried Ruth. 'I'll leave you in Morgan's capable hands, then, Richard, so you can get a real *feel* for what we do. Make sure Morgan gives you a T-shirt before you leave.'

Ruth disappeared. Morgan looked at Richard apprehensively. She'd been surprised at just how upset she'd been by his anger, which still slightly puzzled her—if he'd decided it was funny to be dragged downstream over two miles of sharp rocks, what was so bad about one little black eye? But instead of laughing it off he'd scorched her ears with a sizzling dressing down which had made his remarks about the tyre look positively complimentary.

What was he doing here now? She didn't have to

look far for the easy, obvious answer: he was here for revenge.

'I hope you don't mind if I watch,' Richard said politely. 'I'd like to get a better idea of just how this works.'

The grey eyes met hers; Morgan felt a little prickle at the back of her neck. The last time they'd met he had held her in his arms. . .

Damn him! Just when she needed all her wits about her she felt the unmistakable tug of attraction; she should be working out a strategy for dealing with this suave, presentable menace, and instead. . .

Instead, she realised in exasperation, she was discovering for the first time what the hackneyed old phrase 'mentally undress' actually meant. Her eyes had fastened on the beautifully tied knot of his tie, the immaculately pressed, snugly buttoned collar beneath the smooth, hard line of his jaw, and the image had flashed into her mind of how she might spoil all this, loosening the knot with her fingers, undoing the buttons on the businesslike shirt one by one. . .

You *idiot*, she told herself furiously. She had got to do better than this. She wasn't going to give in without a fight—she would *make* him see how worthwhile it was.

'I'm afraid you *can't* watch,' she said crisply. 'I don't approve of observers in the classroom; it makes everyone self-conscious and interferes with their work. If you'd like to stay you'll have to join in. We're about to start on a geographical mural of the world; why don't you work on South America with Sadeia and Brian?'

'All right,' he said obediently. He unbuttoned his jacket and threw it over a chair, and began rolling up his cuffs in a businesslike way. Morgan dragged her eyes impatiently away from a spectacle uncomfortably close to her fantasy, and turned to the children.

'This is Richard Kavanagh, the presenter and

researcher of a television news programme called
Firing Line. He's going to be working with us today.'

Richard turned to Sadeia and Brian. 'Right, what do
we do next?'

'*I'll* show you,' said Sadeia. 'Come over here—no,
this way. Do you have a felt-tip pen?'

'I'm afraid not.'

'That's all right; you can use one of Brian's.'

He laughed, and Morgan's heart seemed to turn
over; his smile had all its old devastating charm, but
now there was none for her. Sadeia grinned up at him
and led him off.

Just act naturally, Morgan told herself. Pretend he
isn't there. But suddenly her hands were all thumbs,
dropping scissors, breaking chalk, sharpening a pencil
until the lead snapped. Just behave normally, she told
herself feverishly, making her way from Europe to
North America and knocking over four chairs in mid-
Atlantic. She began tidying a table unconvincingly
while ripples of laughter greeted a series of just about
repeatable anecdotes about Brazil.

At last Morgan walked reluctantly down to the
Southern hemisphere, where Richard sat on the floor
surrounded by thirteen giggling children, including
several from Europe, Asia and Australia.

Watching him unobserved, Morgan felt a sudden
flood of relief. He was drawing a sketch of Pelé with
clean, unhurried strokes, tossing out a story about the
Brazilian soccer hero and arguing good-naturedly with
two young supporters of Manchester United—and it
was obvious, beyond any conceivable chance of mistake, that he liked the children. You couldn't fake that
kind of rapport. Whatever his reasons for coming here,
whatever his feelings about their teacher, it was simply
not possible that he could deliberately harm the urchins
now pelting him with questions.

But now, fear dispelled, came awareness.

Richard was sitting sideways to her, his head turned slightly away—a position which accentuated the hard, clean line of his jaw—and Morgan's eyes seemed to zero in of their own accord on the cheek that she had once brushed with her lips. The memory was suddenly so vivid that it was almost as if she could still feel the silky, smooth skin under her mouth.

She should have been doing something...teaching... but she stared at him as if hypnotised, her eyes devouring a thousand forgotten details which she must once have noticed because they struck her now with the shock of recognition: the way his hair was cropped close at the back, the set of his ear, the way his mouth lifted infinitesimally, just at the corner, in a fractional upward curve...

Suddenly he raised his eyes and she was trapped, frozen in that brilliant gaze like a rabbit in the beam of a headlight.

Morgan blushed bright red.

'Just seeing how everyone was getting on,' she babbled, stepped abruptly backwards. The table behind her shuddered, then tilted sharply, folding its unsteady legs like a kneeling camel; drawing pins, paper clips, gold paper stars showered to the floor.

The rest of the afternoon seemed endless, but at last it was four o'clock. Brief chaos engulfed the classroom as materials were put away and surfaces tidied and the children poured out—and then she and Richard were alone.

'I hope you got what you wanted,' Morgan said awkwardly.

'Well, it's a start,' he said. He leant back against her desk, thrusting his hands in his pockets. 'Oh, hell, I've got Brian's felt-tip pen. Of course, it does have sentimental value, being a gift from Sadeia...'

Morgan smiled. 'I'll give it back for you.'

WHAT'S YOUR SIGN?

INSTRUCTIONS

Locate **your** Zodiac Sign above. Carefully detach and stick it in the space provided on your "ZODIAC CHART GAME". These Prize Draw Numbers could be **your** luckiest numbers ever!

GO FOR AN EXTRA £20 FAST CASH - NOW!

Can you find the other half of this £20 voucher? This offer is time sensitive - so be sure to respond <u>NOW</u> - you could be one of 50 drawn who will AUTOMATICALLY receive £20 IN GOOD OLD ENGLISH POUNDS! To play, detach this half of the £20 voucher, moisten it and stick it in the space provided beside the other half.

A short silence fell. He turned the pen idly over in his hands, frowning down at it. Morgan bit her lip; she had been trying for hours not to look at him, but her eyes, yet again, drifted unbidden to his face, then down to the firm, sensual mouth.

Now the mouth curved in a faint, rueful smile. 'I'm sorry I startled you by turning up here.' There was a glint of amusement at her discomfiture, despite his words, in the brilliant eyes which now met hers. 'Elaine wouldn't give me your number so this was the only way I could find you—and I thought I might as well combine business with pleasure.'

'What?' Morgan asked faintly.

'I know I got carried away the other day, but I knew you wouldn't give a damn about something I'd said in the heat of the moment.'

'Oh, I didn't give it a second thought,' Morgan said grittily.

'I'm afraid I leapt to conclusions.' He was wearing, Morgan saw with a flicker of irritation, his not really very worried expression. 'The thing is, it hadn't been all that easy to swallow your somewhat chaotic arrival on the scene as a rescue operation, so when I realised you were the girl at that party...' He shrugged. 'I thought you'd taken a particularly petty revenge on me for emotions you couldn't deal with and wrecked something I'd been working on for months.'

Morgan bit back a retort. Mr Never Apologise was back on form.

'Anyway, I went back along the path later to collect my gear. The camera had been smashed, and there were other signs that there'd been an ambush—if you know anything about guerrilla warfare you get to know what to look for. If I'd known someone was walking into that kind of trap I'd have done my damnedest to get him out pronto.'

Correction, Morgan thought sourly. That *was* the apology.

'Well, I'm glad we've got it all cleared up,' she said carefully.

'And how.' He smiled at her now—the full-voltage Kavanagh smile. 'My God, what a lot of time we've wasted. Remember when we climbed out of the river?'

'Well. . .' began Morgan.

'God, you were beautiful.' The electric eyes held her mesmerised for a moment. 'I couldn't get you out of my mind,' he said, his deep voice caressing her. He smiled again, the smile lighting up his eyes in the way she remembered all too well. He put one hand to her cheek. 'I kept remembering what you'd said. Do you remember?'

Morgan's temper began to stir. 'Do you remember?' In other words, Now I know you were innocent you can go to bed with me, you lucky girl.

'Richard,' she said softly.

'Mmm?'

'I know it's childish to go around blacking people's eyes,' she said sweetly, 'so what do other women do when they don't want you to kiss them?'

'They always want me to kiss them.' He was half joking—but only half. She could feel her cheek go hot under his hand and her pulse quicken; perhaps this thrill was all other women would care about. But he was so *arrogant*. He hadn't even apologised for accusing her of something wicked, and now he just wanted to pick up where they'd left off.

'I'm so glad to hear it,' Morgan said cordially. 'Perhaps we can find one for you on your way out.'

A black eyebrow shot up in astonishment. Didn't anybody *ever* say no?

'Until a few hours ago,' she continued pleasantly, 'you were someone I saw once a week on TV who took a two-year-old black eye as an unforgivable insult. Now it seems it wasn't just a silly old black eye—no, you thought I'd tried to wreck your programme because I was so repressed that I couldn't cope with a perfectly *ordinary* kiss.

'And *now*,' she said, suddenly furious, 'now you realise it was all a mistake, but do you apologise? Oh, no! You just remember you once wondered what it would be like to go to bed with me. Well, you can just go *on* wondering, because all *I* want is to get you this blasted T-shirt and go back to my paperwork.'

She began to walk briskly to the door. Richard muttered something under his breath about T-shirts and followed her, hands thrust into his pockets. But as they stepped into the corridor his eyes met hers.

'So you caught my interview with the head of that Presbyterian sect?' he asked casually.

'Yes—'

'It was a subject that happens to interest you,' he said blandly. 'I don't suppose you bothered with the genetic engineer the other day. . .?'

'Well, as a matter of fact—'

'It was just a subject that happens to interest you?' An eyebrow shot up in mock surprise. 'That's what I like about you, Morgan; you've got such a wide range of interests. Now that arms dealer last week wouldn't be everyone's cup of tea, but something tells me it just happened to be a subject that interests you. . .'

Morgan stalked off down a corridor of ancient, peeling linoleum. He caught up with her effortlessly.

'It's all right, I won't get the wrong idea,' he assured her, the grey eyes dancing. 'I know you're not one of my fans.'

Morgan marched on in silence, gritting her teeth. She'd just told him in no uncertain terms what a self-centred swine he was, and she hadn't even managed to dent that monstrous ego. And the worst of it was that he was right; she *had* watched the programme to see

him, she *had* missed him and wished things hadn't gone
so wrong. But that was when she hadn't had the real
thing getting under her skin. It would serve him right if
she blacked his eye again just for being generally
obnoxious.

She flung open the storeroom door and stopped
abruptly, too late, just inside. In her exasperation she'd
forgotten to insist on Richard waiting in the classroom,
and now he'd followed her in before she could think of
a way to stop him. She turned on the light and suddenly
they were surrounded by hundreds of T-shirts in chic
pastels, stacked in beautiful array on the ceiling-high
shelves.

He gave a low whistle. 'Good Lord, you must have
some marketing operation. I'd no idea.' The speculat-
ive look he cast round the room made Morgan distinctly uneasy; he'd made one of his lightning-quick
changes of gear, and she was no longer alone with
God's gift to British womanhood but with one of the
finest investigative journalists of his generation. She
could almost *see* him assessing the capital tied up in the
room, matching it against the shabby, under-equipped
schoolroom.

'I don't have anything to do with that side of it,'
Morgan said evasively. 'What colour would you like?'

'Let's see; blue seems safe enough. Of course I'll pay
for it; what do I owe you?'

'Seventeen pounds fifty,' said Morgan, pulling one
off the shelf.

An eyebrow flickered upwards. 'That's pretty steep,
isn't it?'

'Well, the marketing strategist thought that was the
right price,' she said, trying not to think of how much
the marketing strategist had been paid. If the figure
didn't come into her mind, he couldn't read it there.
'But you don't have to buy one if you'd rather not.'

'No, that's all right.' He handed her a twenty-pound

note. 'Keep the change; have a couple of felt-tip pens on me.' He took the T-shirt from her, his eyes moving thoughtfully over the walls of merchandise, but made no further comment.

'Would you like to come back to the classroom and see how it all works?' Morgan asked desperately. Anything to get him away.

He looked mildly startled. 'If you're sure you can spare the time.' Morgan remembered, too late, that she'd been trying to throw him out not five minutes ago.

'I'll explain the record-keeping as I go along,' she improvised hastily. At least let him go away with the children—the thing that it was all about—uppermost in his mind.

She shepherded him out of the room, talking continuously until she had him safely back in her own domain. Now she wasn't so sure it was an improvement—those hard, too shrewd grey eyes swept the classroom, homing in on the milk crates used for seats, the ubiquitous recycled computer printouts, the travel posters strategically placed over stains and peeling plaster. But she would *make* him understand.

Shaking off her unease, Morgan outlined some of her methods for dealing with so varied and transient a class, showing the projects being worked on, the children's lockers and logbooks, the system of record-keeping she'd worked out, the worksheets that could be sent to children who'd missed more than a day.

'I send them even if the only contact address we've got is a shelter or a hostel,' she explained. 'Anything to make them feel they're still part of what's going on, that they can always come back.'

'Sounds like a lot of work,' he commented.

Morgan shrugged. She had sat down at her desk and begun stuffing envelopes with worksheets, referring from time to time to the work files of the absentees.

Every file told a story—of a child learning to spell, improving arithmetic, extending his or her knowledge of the natural world. . .and sometimes, after a gap of a month, learning the same thing over again. What ordinary school could allow for that?

Richard had propped himself on one arm to look over her shoulder. At first, though she wasn't looking at him, she felt abnormally aware of him—but as he put one question after another she gradually lost her self-consciousness and found herself telling anecdotes about the children, sharing some of the successes and set-backs of her rather unorthodox classroom.

And at some point she realised, in astonishment, that she was actually enjoying herself. It wasn't just that she was defending A Child's Place against a possible enemy; she was sharing with Richard the thing that mattered most to her.

'It's pretty amazing what you've managed to do,' he remarked, and for once there was not a trace of irony in the dark, clever face. He grinned ruefully. 'But at this rate you'll be here all night. I'm sorry I've taken up so much of your time—' He broke off and stared incredulously at his watch. 'Oh, *hell*.'

'What is it?' asked Morgan.

'It's seven-thirty and I'm supposed to be meeting Elaine half an hour ago across town. I'll have to call her from the car.' He raised a quizzical eyebrow. 'I don't want to take too much for granted, but can I tell her we're on speaking terms?'

Morgan looked up at him and smiled sweetly. 'For the time being,' she said.

'*Darling*,' said Richard. He snatched up his T-shirt and dashed for the door.

CHAPTER EIGHT

MORGAN didn't know much about how the research for *Firing Line* was organised, but she was rather surprised by how much time Richard seemed to spend at the school in the next few weeks. And, even when he wasn't there, as like as not he would call to ask if she could meet him for dinner 'to fill me in on a few points'.

The invitations were tongue-in-cheek, so she had no real right to complain if the 'few points' remained decidedly vague. But, given that they weren't really about business, it was, she sometimes thought, all the more worrying that these dinners were decidedly addictive.

They argued about everything under the sun.

Morgan knew perfectly well that the exhilaration she felt in crossing swords with Richard had nothing to do with her love of a good argument. Even now, when she'd spent hours in his company, she hadn't really got used to the sheer magnetism of the black-browed face with its blazing eyes and sensual mouth. She still felt a queer shock when her eyes met his; when she scored a point—not as often as she'd have liked—he threw his head back and laughed, and the blood seemed to race in her veins.

There was no point in pretending that Richard didn't know it perfectly well too. There was a spark of amusement in his eyes when he gave her those deliberate, devastating smiles, as if he knew full well their effect on her. But he did nothing about it. He always saw her home, and saw her to her door, but left without so much as a kiss on the cheek.

Despising herself, Morgan spent hours trying to work

out what it meant. Did it mean a) he didn't want to
sleep with her after all because it would mean more of
a commitment than he was ready for? b) he wanted to
get to know her first because it really meant something
to him? c) he wanted to wait until she was ready, and
was waiting for her to make the first move? or d) he
was just being bloody-minded?

Most of the time she plumped for d), either on its
own or possibly in combination with one of the other
three. But it didn't matter. She'd long ago stopped
suspecting his motives for coming to A Child's Place—
how could you suspect someone who invariably came
to the classroom with a box of supplies that had 'fallen
off the back of a lorry'? And she had to face the fact
that her heart leapt when she heard his voice on the
phone, or even heard his feet in the corridor—and that
life would seem stale, flat and unprofitable without
him.

Morgan had reached this rather worrying conclusion,
and was attacking an even knottier problem—was she
actually going to have to work up the courage to make
a pass at Richard?—when Richard drove her home
after yet another dinner one evening. He had been
unusually withdrawn, but suddenly he broke the silence
with an unexpected question.

'Am I right in thinking none of the children is
literally sleeping on the streets?' he asked. 'The cardboard box is more of a crowd-stopper?'

'Yes,' admitted Morgan. 'I mean, it's not that there
aren't children living in cardboard boxes, and I only
wish they *would* come—but we'd really need to provide
transportation to make it feasible. Ruth keeps saying
we'll get a van, but it hasn't materialised so far.'

'Mmm.' The streetlights chiselled his face into harsh
contours. 'I know money's pretty tight. Though I'd
have thought with Innismere Conglomerates as a sponsor that you could rise to one lousy van. . .'

'I know,' said Morgan. 'But apparently they're just funding our publicity materials.'

'I see.' After a short pause he added, 'Well, God knows that can mount up. You wouldn't happen to know when they came on board?'

Morgan narrowed her eyes, trying to remember. 'A couple of years ago? I can't really remember. Ruth's always telling me how poor we are, you see; it's her way of keeping the teachers from being extravagant with supplies. So she might not have told me the exact date we got a corporate sponsor—she might have been worried there'd be a run on pencils if I thought we were rich.'

'I see,' he said again. There was a rather longer pause this time as he negotiated the warren of streets off Bow Road and at last pulled up by Morgan's house. 'Morgan. . .' he began at last.

'Yes?' she prompted him.

He reached suddenly across to take her hand. 'I like you very much, Morgan,' he said, looking down at the long, slender fingers rather than at her face.

'And I like you,' said Morgan, realising, to her surprise, that it was true.

'I'd like to go on seeing you,' he went on. 'But something's come up—something I've got to look into. I've no idea what it will take to get to the bottom of it, and that's on top of the usual three-ring circus of getting the programme on the air every week. So I may not be able to call you for a few weeks. If that happens, I don't want you to think I'm giving you the run-around. I'll get in touch as soon as I possibly can.'

'All right,' said Morgan. She couldn't quite make out his expression.

He hesitated, as if about to say something more, then got out of the car abruptly to see her to the door.

Morgan couldn't see that she was likely to be in any danger that she couldn't handle between the car and the door, but she found she was unaccountably reluctant to say goodbye. She got out of the car and walked demurely to the door by his side.

He stood silently beside her for a moment, looking down at her.

Morgan screwed up her courage. 'Would you like to come in?' she asked bluntly.

'And do what?' he asked rather edgily.

Oh, good, he was picking a fight. Anything was better than this distance, this feeling that she would be miserable the moment his car disappeared from view. 'Talk?' she said. 'Drink nasty, cheap instant coffee? Watch sheepdog trials on the box? Play Scrabble? The choice is endless.'

He didn't pick up the bait, but he did at least snap out of his brown study. 'Well, the sheepdog trials are a draw,' he said, 'but I'd better be going.'

Morgan realised that she would feel a complete idiot saying, You can kiss me goodnight. She remembered how easily Elaine had raised her mouth to meet his— but that casual, easy movement was beyond her too. Suddenly she smiled up at him.

'Well, how about a goodnight kiss to show there are no hard feelings?' she said, her low voice husky with shyness.

'Oh, *Morgan*,' he said with something like a groan, and the next moment she was in his arms.

The last time, a combination of powerful emotions had made his kisses hard and ruthless. Now his arms held her tightly against him but his mouth was tender, coaxing her to open hers. Her mouth parted for the velvety softness of his tongue, the tip of hers meeting his with an electric shock that made her quiver.

She lost track of time in the heady intoxication of his embrace, pressing closer and closer against him, returning kiss for kiss. At some point he sank down to half sit on the iron railing, pulling her forward to stand

between his lean, muscular thighs, and she sank against
him, feeling that she could happily have stayed there
for ever.

Far too soon he raised his head. 'Does your invitation
still stand?'

Morgan hesitated. Before she'd known Richard it
would never have occurred to her that, all her other
feelings about a man being a mass of contradictions,
the one thing she could be sure of was that she desired
him. She would also have rejected out of hand someone
who had cold-bloodedly said that he wanted to go to
bed with her to see what it was like.

She closed her eyes, feeling the solid brick of the
house under her hand. Her mind was in turmoil, her
feelings in complete confusion; but at least if she did
nothing she would have nothing to regret. She opened
her eyes and looked at him doubtfully, trying to bring
her breathing under control.

'I take it that means no,' he said, rising to his feet
and thrusting his hands in his pockets. 'Wonderful.'

Morgan wondered whether she would ever get used
to having her temper so close to the surface. She had
always been so easygoing, so tolerant, so good-
humoured! But whenever she was around Richard she
seemed to veer bewilderingly from anger to passion to
wild laughter and back again. Now exasperation made
her say dampeningly, 'I thought you *wanted* to kiss me.
I'm sorry you had something forced on you you didn't
want. It's absolutely terrible to come up against a
person of immensely superior strength.'

He opened his mouth and shut it again. His quicksilver
eyes crackled with more than one kind of frustration.

'It was *lovely*,' he said, and paused. He raised one
bold black eyebrow. 'The perfect end to a perfect day.'

He flicked her cheek with a finger and strode down
the walk to the car.

* * *

Three weeks passed. Morgan caught *Firing Line* every Friday, but had no closer contact with its presenter. Well, he'd said he'd be busy. And then the three weeks became four, and then five, and then six, and still Morgan heard nothing from Richard.

Probably, she told herself, he had meant what he'd said at the time—but there were lots of women in the world, and probably one had been standing by for when he first had a minute to spare. They didn't have that much in common—in fact, they had nothing in common, so she'd do better to put him out of her mind.

She'd come to this sensible conclusion for the fourth time in as many days when Friday came round. Time for *Firing Line*. Not, perhaps, the thing best calculated to put Richard out of her mind, but from force of habit Morgan turned on her television.

The familiar music came on. Richard walked onto the set and sat down. And now, to her astonishment, another familiar figure walked on stage, immaculately groomed and coiffed: Ruth!

Morgan stared at the screen in perplexity. Even if Richard hadn't had time for a date, why hadn't he called to tell her that the Child's Place programme was to be shown? Well, she thought wryly, probably he took it for granted that she always watched the show. And she settled down to watch.

The interview began by covering the aims of A Child's Place. There was filmed footage of the charity itself, a shot of the presenter of *Firing Line*, armed with felt-tip pens, decorating a map of Brazil under instruction from an imperious seven-year-old girl—'Not like *that*, silly; can't you do anything right?' Morgan grinned; she could imagine viewers across Britain bursting into laughter—and, she hoped, reaching for their cheque-books.

But as the narrative went on her smile faded. Now Richard was asking Ruth where the money came from, probing the delicate subject of the marketing strategy. Morgan looked at him suspiciously. She had seen that serious, responsible look too often to think it boded anything but ill for Ruth and A Child's Place.

Ruth might think that if she could somehow put paid to this inconvenient line of questioning she would be home free—but they were only fifteen minutes into the programme. If he'd decided to take this line, he must have something bigger—and worse—up his sleeve; right now he was just softening Ruth up, breaking her nerve, getting bloodthirsty viewers on his side, waiting for Ruth to crack.

It was almost a relief when it came. Almost. As Morgan stared wide-eyed at the screen Richard revealed that Innismere Conglomerates had paid for a hundred thousand pounds' worth of publicity materials for A Child's Place, which had been commissioned from PRpr—who had paid thirty thousand pounds to Ruth Everett-Davies for a report on the multicultural classroom. Another two hundred and fifty thousand pounds had gone on a marketing strategy with designer products from The Market, who had paid Ruth Everett-Davies sixty thousand pounds for a series of seminars on breaking the glass ceiling. And the list went on...

Blood roared in Morgan's ears. It had to be true. She knew Ruth, and she knew Richard. He was unspeakable—just how unspeakable she'd never realised until now—but he got his facts right. And because he'd revealed this publicly—because he'd given the school no chance to replace Ruth—he'd ensured a scandal from which a charity so small and vulnerable could never recover. In no time at all the doors of A Child's Place would close and the children would have nowhere to go.

A surge of rage burst through her. Ruth would leave the studio, and Richard, no doubt, would shrug and go

home to bed and get up the next day and be onto the
next thing. Well, she wouldn't let him off so easily. She
had to see him.

The weekend was sheer hell. Elaine flatly refused to
divulge either Richard's home address or telephone
number, and Morgan was forced to relieve her feelings
by sending a vitriolic letter to the studio letting him
know just what she thought of him. Monday was no
better: she called Richard at the studio, but his secretary had by then opened the vitriolic letter and
refused to put her through.

She would have to go to the studio in person.

It took three days to find a substitute who could take
her class. But on Thursday Morgan set out for the
suburb from which Richard and Elaine broadcast to
the British public.

She presented herself at the gate of the studio at
eleven a.m., explaining with aplomb that she had come
to see Elaine Roberts. Reception called Elaine, who
admitted to having a sister and to being prepared to
see her. Armed with a visitor's pass, Morgan proceeded
to the lifts.

ROBERTS E was on the second floor. KAVANAGH R was
on the fifth. Morgan coolly ascended to the fifth floor,
and began making her way down a long corridor, trying
to look as if she knew where she was going.

The office numbers began to approach that of her
quarry. Morgan stalked into a secretary's small cubicle
outside an office.

'Is Richard Kavanagh in?' she asked curtly.

A competent-looking brunette looked up from her
word processor. 'Yes, but I'm afraid he can't see you
now. Would you like to wait or leave a message?'
Morgan turned to the door. 'You can't go in there!'
shrieked the girl.

'Watch me,' said Morgan, opening it with a flourish.

She strode in as if through the doors of a Wild West saloon and stopped, hands on hips, just inside. There were two men in the room, one a Very Important Person it might once have excited her to meet. She ignored him.

'How could you?' she said in a harsh, grating voice, glaring at his companion. 'How *could* you? You bloody *coward*! You self-serving, self-righteous, self-congratulating *coward*!'

The girl at the desk had rushed into the room after her, and now grabbed her arm. 'I'm sorry, Richard,' she panted. 'I tried to stop her and she just went right in.'

'You're damned right I did,' said Morgan, shaking off the arm. 'Mr Kavanagh seems to have an aversion to the telephone. Mr Kavanagh finds it convenient to have someone answer his letters for him, so I've just received *this—*' her voice dripped scorn as she held up a form letter '—in the post.

'"Dear Ms Roberts,"' she read out sarcastically. '"Please forgive this form letter, which the size of our mailbag makes necessary. We are sorry that you were distressed by the programme. *Firing Line* deals with controversial issues, and inevitably viewers may disagree with our conclusions, but I can assure you that every effort is made to ensure factual accuracy. If an error was made, please let us know, providing relevant documentation, and a full and public retraction will be made."'

'Bloody *hell*!' She tore the letter viciously in half, in fours, and then in eighths, and threw the fragments to the floor. 'You unspeakable *hypocrite*!'

Richard had seemed nailed to the spot, but at this he came to life again. 'Viv, take Sir Roger down to Terry's office and give him a coffee, will you? I'll be with you as soon as I can.'

The door closed behind the two onlookers. Morgan

continued to stare implacably at Richard. She opened
her mouth again, but he cut her off.

'Just a moment, Morgan. Unless you can say what
you've got to say in two minutes flat I don't have time
to listen to it. This is between the two of us, but there
are other people involved in the programme and I can't
let you hijack it. I'm not sure what good it will do, but
I'm prepared to meet you later if there's something
more you want to say.'

Morgan stared at him as if she'd never seen him
before. Seeing him calm, composed, businesslike and
completely unashamed, she wondered whether there
was any point in talking. But why should he be allowed
to ruin people's lives—*children's* lives, and children
who had nowhere else to turn—and then shelter behind
a secretary and a barricade of form letters? 'Where?'
she said grittily.

He thought for a moment. 'Things are pretty hectic
the day before the day, but I'll try to get away by eight.
As for where—well, we can have a late dinner at a
restaurant I know, but if you just want to hurl abuse at
me we'd better find a park bench. The choice is yours.'

Morgan clenched her fists. 'I don't believe this,' she
said. 'I don't believe you're human.' She raised her
chin defiantly. 'I'll meet you at the restaurant.'

'Fine.' He took a card from a pocket and scrawled
something on the back. 'I'll try to be on time, but if I'm
late don't give up on me; I'll be there one way or
another. I've given you my home address and phone
number in case you need to get in touch with me—if
you call me here the person who gets the flak is Viv,
which really doesn't make a hell of a lot of sense.'

Morgan took the card and slipped it into a pocket.

'I'll see you at eight-thirty, then,' said Richard.

'All right,' said Morgan. She turned and walked out
of the room.

She took the train back into town with some vague

thought of spending the day doing the things she'd always planned to do when she had the time—visit a museum, perhaps see a film—but her heart was too heavy, and she ended by walking aimlessly for hours.

At first she flinched every time she passed a news-stand, expecting to see Ruth's shame emblazoned across the front pages. But A Child's Place had no glamorous patrons, no one had been caught having an affair with anyone else, and, in fact, the catastrophe which had brought her world crashing down was relegated to a couple of column inches deep inside the more serious papers.

She was early at the restaurant—a small Italian bistro in Fulham—but Richard had reserved a table. She ordered a gin and tonic and sat drinking this and eating breadsticks, taking a mild satisfaction in the sharp crack with which they broke. And at about eight forty-five Richard walked into the restaurant.

She watched him pause by the till for a word with the owner, then cross the room with his long, easy stride. He sank into the chair opposite her a little heavily and leant back in it, resting his forearms on the edge of the table and lacing his fingers together. She saw, with cool detachment, that he looked tired; perhaps he wouldn't have it all his own way with his next victim.

'Hello, Morgan,' he said quietly. 'Do you want another drink?'

She shook her head.

'Do you know what you're having?' she nodded. 'Shall we sort that out now, then?' He made a sign to the waiter, who approached, pad at the ready. The orders were quickly given, and the waiter withdrew with the menus.

Before she could decide what to say first he spoke. 'I'm sorry you couldn't get through to me,' he said in the same quiet, controlled voice. 'And I really am sorry about that damned form letter; of course you weren't meant to get that. I should have got in touch earlier.' His fingers drummed on the table. 'I suppose there didn't seem to be a lot to say. But that was really for you to decide, after all.'

Morgan took a breath; it seemed suddenly to be something that she consciously had to remember to do. 'Is that all you have to say?' she said.

'You're the one who wanted to talk,' he pointed out. 'I don't like the way things have turned out, but I can't think of anything I could say that would improve matters. But I'm prepared to listen to anything you want to say.'

Morgan stared at him. 'Don't you have any idea of what you've done?' Her voice was barely audible.

'I have a fair idea, yes.' His face was impassive. She would have been furious if he'd tried to manipulate the conversation with his usual panache, but she found this complete lack of resistance oddly hard to deal with.

'And you're not sorry?' she asked incredulously.

His eyes met hers steadily. 'If you mean am I sorry the school will have to close—yes, I am. But if you mean do I wish things were just as they were, with the school a handy little concern for your chief to milk for all it's worth—no, I don't. I'd do it again today.'

'But—' she made a helpless gesture with her hand '—I thought you *liked* the children. You showed that film-clip with Sadeia; what do you think will happen to her? Don't you care? Or were you planning to send her a set of pens as a consolation prize?'

At last she had pricked him slightly. 'Of course I liked them,' he said wearily. 'I liked you. I still do. What do you want me to do—rob a bank to prove it?' The impatience died down as quickly as it had flared up. 'Look, something like eighty per cent of charities' income comes from about a fifth of the population. In other words, you don't get people suddenly becoming generous when they see a really worthwhile new cause—you've got competition for pieces of a fixed pie.'

'I'm well aware of that—' Morgan began.

'And your director,' he went on patiently, 'was not only spectacularly dishonest but grotesquely incompetent. So if you keep her in business to give Sadeia twenty-five pence in the pound, that's seventy-five pence in every pound of donation that's going on crazy marketing schemes instead of to three other children you don't happen to know—children who could be helped by a properly run charity if they got the money.'

'I never said *Ruth* should stay—' Morgan began.

'The place stood and fell with Ruth,' he said with a shrug. 'If there'd been someone who could take over at the top I might have gone about this differently.'

'Discreetly, you mean?' Morgan sneered. 'It wouldn't have been much of a story, would it?'

'The trustees had been hand-picked not to interfere,' he pointed out. 'She'd made damn sure there was no number two... You've got to face facts, Morgan. There was no way to keep the place going without her.'

The waiter placed a plate in front of Morgan. She looked at it as if she had never seen spaghetti before, then ignored it.

'Of course I didn't expect you to see it that way,' added Richard while the waiter put down his order then withdrew. 'I realise you're emotionally involved with these particular children.'

'Yes,' Morgan said curtly. 'Whereas you're not emotionally involved with anyone, are you, Richard?'

For once Richard had nothing to say.

'Would it have made any difference if you'd come in that night?'

There was a very long pause while Richard turned over this impossible question. 'It would have made it

harder to do the right thing,' he said at last. 'My guess
is the net result would have been the same. So it's just
as well you played safe, isn't it?'

He grimaced at her bleak face and added, 'I think I
was right, but if you think there's anything I can do
now. . .'

Morgan pulled herself together. 'Yes,' she said
crisply. 'There is something you can do. You can tell
your father you've become interested in science and
would like a new lab, and could you please have a
hundred thousand pounds. Then you can give it to me,
and then you can go to hell. I believe that will be
adequate for present requirements, if you really want
to do something.'

For the first time since he'd arrived something like
amusement crossed his face. 'Morgan, you're about
eight years too late. My mother told him about our
little game as a kind of parting shot, and he hasn't
given me a penny since. He doesn't trust me.'

'And who can blame him?' said Morgan.

He shrugged. 'He wants it to come to me some day,
but on his conditions. It's all tied up in a bizarre trust
he thought up—I get it if I marry, after the birth of my
first child. I know how dedicated you are, Morgan, but
something tells me even you would shrink from the
ultimate sacrifice.'

Morgan shuddered.

He gave a wry smile. 'Quite.'

She looked down at her plate. 'So there's absolutely
nothing to be done—is that what you're saying?' she
asked.

'Not that I can see. I'm sorry.'

She looked up. 'Well, you're wrong,' she said. She
cast about desperately in her mind, trying to think of
the worst thing she could say to him. There must be
some way she could hurt him. At last she found it.

'You like to think this was the only way, but I don't

believe a word of it. I'm sure Ruth could have been dealt with without destroying the school, but you wanted to humiliate her publicly.'

Her eyes blazed with contempt. 'You didn't like her reminding you that your success might not come from sheer ability, because you want to believe this image you've built up of someone tough, unflinching—the scourge of society... *I* think you saw you could get revenge on her, and you took it, no matter what got in the way. *I* think you had to show how tough you are by smashing something to bits.'

She couldn't tell whether she was hurting him as she wanted to, for the grey eyes merely stared at her impassively.

'But you're not going to get away with it, Richard,' she said, rising to her feet. 'You're not going to win this time. I'm *damned* if you are.'

She pushed her chair back from the table and strode from the restaurant, leaving behind her an untouched plate of spaghetti, and Richard Kavanagh staring silently, sombrely into space.

CHAPTER NINE

A MILD summer breeze stirred the trees in Hyde Park; a limpid July sun flooded the lobby of a block of luxury flats on Park Lane.

Morgan paused halfway across an acre of carpet and surreptitiously eased an aching foot from a high-heeled shoe. It couldn't have been more than half a mile from the bus stop—how strange to think that as little as a month ago she'd always worn the kind of shoes in which half a mile was *only* half a mile. Well, at least she'd be able to sit down in the meeting.

Delaying the moment of putting on her shoe, she glanced at her reflection in one of the vast mirrors which lined the lobby from floor to ceiling. It was an image which should have given satisfaction—she'd certainly worked at it hard enough.

The great mass of dark hair was swept up into an intricate chignon, not loose enough to be untidy, not tight enough to look hard. Below this, her subtle make-up emphasised the large grey eyes, the strong bones; the face looked acute, intelligent—yet passionate and committed. And below this again—oh, torment of torments!—a tailored suit with a narrow, knee-length skirt, and the diabolical shoes.

But they were perfect. The cut of the jacket was severe, but its colour was a soft, deep blue, and the detailing of buttons and pockets was pretty rather than coldly practical. The effect, in short, was of an efficient woman, emphatically of the business world—but one who would never, never, never in a million years line her own pockets at the expense of poor little homeless children.

118

For the past month Morgan had been presenting this image to sponsors, the Charity Commission, the law, the Press, and trustees. Especially trustees. The powers that be had provisionally agreed to the instalment of Miss Roberts as 'caretaker administrator' until a proper appointment of a director could be made—but only if the trustees took their responsibilities a good deal more seriously than they had under the previous regime.

The trustees, however, were smarting from the criticism they'd received over the affair; they were more than half inclined to pack the whole thing in, and required constant soothing on the one hand, and on the other to be talked through accounts which they were quite unable to understand. None of them found it convenient to go to meetings in the East End, so she'd been summoned today to a gathering in Brenda Vavasour's flat.

Wincing, Morgan slipped her foot back into the shoe and made her way carefully to the lift. Heavy metal doors opened silently, then closed behind her, and the lift shot to the top of the building.

A uniformed maid answered the door to Brenda's flat, and showed Morgan immediately to the dining room, which had been turned into an impromptu meeting room. This in itself was a surprise, since the trustees seemed to think that they should be fashionably late for meetings; but she had barely had time to take in the full cast of characters round the table, their strange punctuality, when she realised that there was an addition to their number.

Richard Kavanagh was sitting at Brenda Vavasour's right hand.

His face looked thinner than the last time she'd seen him, and the old faintly cynical look, which had always been leavened with humour, seemed to have hardened into something colder and more bitter. But he still

made everyone else in the room look insignificant—not
that there was, in this case, much competition.

Morgan's heart sank as she glanced round the table;
eight wealthy nonentities were gazing at him, dazzled,
with the same flattered, trusting faces they'd once
turned upon Ruth, as eager as children for a promised
treat.

Now Brenda was rushing into speech. 'The most
marvellous thing, Morgan!' she gushed. 'Richard is
taking three months' leave from *Firing Line* to handle
PR and development on a consultancy basis!' She
checked herself briefly at Morgan's sceptical face, but
took courage from the expectant look of the other
trustees. 'The thing is, Morgan, we're all very grateful
for what you've done, but when it comes right down to
it there's nothing like using a professional.'

'Professional what?' asked Morgan acidly.

'Troubleshooter,' said Richard. 'Aka media hit man.'
The old mocking glint was back in his eyes, but his
voice was all matter-of-fact professionalism. 'Your big
problem is that the place is now a byword for inefficiency and corruption—'

'Thanks to you,' Morgan said sweetly.

The trustees looked shocked. Richard, to her annoyance, only looked amused. 'I think your director had
something to do with it, don't you?' he asked, raising a
quizzical eyebrow.

Not to mention present company. Morgan had herself far too well under control to say it, but the gleaming
look in Richard's eyes showed that one person in the
room knew what she was thinking.

'I know you've done what you could to get the word
out that there's a new sheriff in town,' he went on,
unperturbed, 'but you don't have any contacts and you
don't know how the media operate—*and* you're trying
to do everything else at the same time.' There wasn't
so much as a ripple in the smooth, honeyed voice to

suggest that some of those at the table might take
something on.

'You could waste two months setting up obscure
little press conferences and photo-calls that nobody
comes to, or fishing for endorsements from minor
actors in old TV series.' He tossed a sheet of paper
down the table. 'This is what I have in mind—which
frankly you couldn't organise in two years, let alone
two months.'

Morgan looked at it reluctantly. It was a rough
timetable for various events—a jazz evening, a private
reception in one of the national museums, even an
event in the House of Commons—coupled with a
dazzling list of celebrities who could be prevailed on to
attend.

On the back was an agenda relating to legislation
affecting the homeless and children's welfare, coupled
with all the activities being planned by every other
charity promoting either the homeless or children in
London and at national level, and at the bottom were
comments on how A Child's Place should work with or
around them. No wonder the trustees looked so
thrilled—they probably imagined themselves rubbing
shoulders with a whole galaxy of superstars.

'Very impressive,' Morgan said drily. 'But could I
just remind everyone that this isn't the first time Mr
Kavanagh has come to A Child's Place with an appealing scheme for giving it publicity? Last time he cost us
a quarter of our donors; what conceivable reason do
we have to take him at face value now?'

She saw that the trustees looked unconvinced and
said impatiently, 'I'm sure he *could* do all this and
more. He could just as easily undo all I've—all we've
managed to salvage in the past few weeks. We'd have
to be mad to offer him the opportunity on a plate.'

To her fury the trustees merely looked embarrassed

by this outspokenness. 'Morgan's been under a lot of strain lately, Richard,' Brenda said apologetically.

'It's a fair point,' said Richard magnanimously. 'And she's quite right to be worried if there's anything to hide. Is there?' The grey eyes challenged Morgan.

'Of course not!' Morgan snapped back.

'Then that's all right—' began Brenda.

'No, it is not all right,' Morgan said bluntly. 'We can't pretend the finances are anything but chaotic; it would be child's play for a hostile observer to make the school out to be a hopeless cause. At the moment we have the best possible reason for thinking Mr Kavanagh just such a hostile observer, and I for one don't want to gamble the children's future on his change of heart.'

At this point another voice was heard. 'My dear Morgan!' It was Colonel James Fitzwilliam. 'We'd no idea what Ruth was up to; Kavanagh was quite right to bring it out into the open. As far as we're concerned, he's just the man to get the place back on its feet again; we've no doubts at to his intentions—no doubts at all.

'But of course you must feel free to say if working with him will be a problem for you. We don't want to force you into anything; if you're not comfortable with the idea we can always bring someone in to take over from you and give Kavanagh whatever support he needs.'

Morgan stared round the table while the other trustees avoided her eyes. She tried to imagine what would happen to the charity, left defenceless to Richard's prying eyes; well, he wouldn't destroy it if she could help it. 'No,' she said grittily. 'It won't be a problem.'

There was a little murmur of relief at having got this uncomfortable moment over, and the meeting quickly descended into the disorganised free-for-all that was so familiar to Morgan, with various trustees throwing out bright ideas. It was soon obvious, however, that

Richard had little patience for this pastime — and, unlike Morgan, no need to put up with it.

He interrupted after about five minutes. 'Well, I can see you've got some interesting ideas,' he said. 'But what I really need to do is talk to Morgan about the state of play.'

The hard grey eyes swept round the table. 'Does anyone have any contacts or any specific piece of information which would be a help with the events I've already got lined up?' he asked crisply. 'No? Then I don't think I need to keep you any longer. Brenda, I'm not sure how long I'll need the room, but we should be done by four.'

In Morgan's experience the trustees could talk about nothing for hours, but they responded instantly to the voice of authority, leaving the room without a murmur of protest.

Richard came lazily round the table to stand by Morgan's side, his eyes gleaming with amusement at her predicament.

Morgan looked at him stonily. She'd never realised that it could actually hurt to look at someone, but just the sight of that dark, charismatic face seemed to tear her apart. She knew now what he was like; he'd cold-bloodedly put the scoring of a minor coup ahead of the welfare of children who would never know a fraction of the advantages he'd had.

Yet she was still, in spite of everything, acutely aware of the physical magnetism of the man standing beside her — of the loose-limbed, easy grace of the powerful body, the almost shocking perfection of the hawk-like face. Worst of all, somehow, was the fact that it seemed to go beyond a purely sexual response.

As she registered almost automatically his character-istic expressions, the familiar modulations of the drawl-ing, seductive voice, with each little jolt of recognition she felt something horribly like possessiveness; it was as if, on some primitive level beyond the reach of reason, something inside said, This belongs to me.

Well, that would have been preposterous even if he hadn't behaved unforgivably. He wouldn't have been hers even if she'd wanted him. Elaine had got the coveted place on *Firing Line* a couple of weeks ago, and the papers had been full of the dynamic duo, who apparently had much more than their professional interests in common—not that you could believe everything you read, but there was no obvious reason why collaborating on *Firing Line* required them to hit the hot spots of London every night of the week except one.

'What are you doing here?' she asked.

'Joining a sinking ship, by the look of things,' he said flippantly. 'See how you've misjudged me?' He gave her a rather mocking look. 'You don't seem very pleased to see me. Funny, last time we met I thought you wanted me to make amends.'

'And you said there was nothing you could do,' Morgan reminded him. 'So what *are* you doing here, Richard?'

'Well, let's see. Elaine did get the number-two spot on *Firing Line*, as you may have heard, and I told the studio it would be a good idea to let her find her feet without me breathing down her neck. Everybody got very excited—I think they thought I was about to visit the guerrilla camps that got left out the first time round—and I said, *Firing Line*'s got a terrible reputation for being negative and destructive; why don't I go and patch up A Child's Place and come back with a story about it? And everybody stopped looking excited and said, "How worthwhile."'

He gave her a lazy smile. 'I'd obviously gone stark, staring mad, you see. It was safer to humour me.'

Morgan gritted her teeth. 'Really,' she said sarcastically. 'Richard, you may have pulled the wool over the trustees' eyes, but do you expect me to believe you're

serious about this? I don't care how brilliant you are;
you can't organize a programme like this with no
money—*you* know that even if they don't.'

'All taken care of.' Richard locked his hands behind
his head and grinned at her. 'I used my powers of
persuasion on the trustees, and they've given me twenty
thousand pounds to play with—all out of their own
pockets. So if there are no further questions—'

'Twenty thousand pounds!' Morgan stared at him.
What it came down to was that people who knew
nothing about business, who'd passed all Ruth's sugges-
tions on the nod had decided that they were uneasy
about Morgan and that they'd be happier putting in
someone who knew as little about actually running a
business as they did themselves. 'I'm surprised they
didn't just make you director and have done with it,'
she said bitterly.

'Well, they did offer,' said Richard. 'But I declined. I
wouldn't know the first thing about running a charity.
No, I take that back. The first thing is you don't run off
with the money; I've worked that one out, which puts
me ahead of your dear departed chief.'

'How can you joke about it?' Morgan demanded
fiercely.

He raised an eyebrow in mock astonishment. 'How
can you *not*? The whole place is a farce, Morgan, and
will be as long as that lot have the final say in how it's
run.'

He gave a short laugh. 'I ran into Brenda at a dinner
party, and I gathered from what she said that you were
holding the place together—just. No hard feelings from
that quarter—she was too busy falling over herself
explaining all the safeguards they'd put in place to
make sure *you* didn't rob the place blind. Lucky for
you, my motives *are* pure—it never occurred to her
that *I* might not be trustworthy. One little hint and she
was ready to let me walk in and do whatever I liked.'

Morgan glared at him. 'What did you do—smile nicely?' she asked sarcastically.

'Trade secret.' He gave her a sardonic smile. 'My heart went out to you, struggling on all alone but for the odd trustee to explain things to in words of one syllable. And I've always liked a challenge. I had a hankering to see if I couldn't put Humpty Dumpty back together again. And I'd liked what I'd seen of the school; it would be a shame if it went under—which it probably would if I didn't give you a hand. . .'

Morgan clenched her fists. 'How *dare* you?' she exclaimed. 'How dare you come here and talk about it being a good thing—?'

The amusement had melted from his face, leaving it unusually stern. 'Quite easily, as it happens,' he said coolly, his eyes steely. 'I don't equate caring for the school with covering up for someone who was siphoning off most of its money, and I'm damned if I'll apologise for my hypocrisy when I'm about to raise some money to put in its place.'

He looked at her unsmilingly. 'Of course there's more to it than that. We were attracted to each other and thinking of doing something about it; you seem to think it's some kind of insult if I come here and brazen it out as if nothing happened. I thought I was giving you credit for having your priorities straight.

'I know you think that programme was a personal betrayal, quite apart from the fact that it hurt something you cared about; well, I took it for granted we couldn't be involved on a personal level now, but I also took it for granted that you'd want my help if I could do things for the school that you couldn't.'

Morgan bit her lip. The sore, angry feeling at the offhand words about personal involvement just proved that he was right—she was letting her emotions interfere with what was best for the children.

'Well?' he insisted ruthlessly.

'I do,' Morgan forced herself to say.

His manner changed abruptly to one of brisk practicality. 'Right,' he said coolly, folding his arms across his chest. 'Now, as far as I can tell you've spent the past month licking your wounds. It's not good enough. You've got to fight fire with fire, make sure people hear enough good things about the place to wipe out the programme, and when I say people I mean the right people. I've wangled invitations to a few things, and more should be coming in any day; it's time to start getting out and about.'

He handed her another agenda—this time a list of dinners and lunches, cocktail parties and receptions hosted by people Morgan hadn't thought anybody actually knew personally.

She glanced at it and handed it back. 'Richard, if you want to go to these things that's fine, but I'd really rather not go myself. I simply can't spare the time. There's an enormous amount of work to do; I don't think you understand—'

'No, *you* don't understand,' he interrupted. 'It doesn't matter how tight a ship you run if nobody knows about it. You need to be out there building up support. *You* need to be there, if only because you know more about it than anyone else. We'll have to do something about your clothes, of course—'

'No, we won't,' Morgan said edgily. 'I wouldn't know what to say, even if I had a millionaire as a captive audience.'

'I know you wouldn't,' was the unexpected reply. 'I've seen you when you thought you had a guilty secret. You don't just walk into something like that; I'd brief you, of course.' He looked at her thoughtfully. 'Somebody asks you what you do and you say you work for A Child's Place. And they say, "A Child's Place! But isn't that the place that was exposed by *Firing Line*?" What do you say? Or do you just try to change the subject and leave the room the first chance you get?'

Morgan gritted her teeth. 'I—I suppose I'd say yes, it was, but Ruth wasn't there any more and we—I—we were doing the best we could to—'

'What you say,' he interposed coolly, 'is, "Yes, that's absolutely right, and I was the one who got Richard Kavanagh interested in the charity. Now that the director's gone he's spearheading a campaign to raise funds for the school; would you like to come to our reception at the House of Commons in the autumn?" Got that?'

Morgan nodded dumbly.

'Let's hear it, then. And what do you do?' he asked, his voice shifting abruptly from brisk efficiency to polite lack of interest.

'I work for A Child's Place,' Morgan said mechanically.

'A Child's Place?' If she hadn't been so furious she'd have been amused by the sudden spark of recognition, the double take, the beautifully timed pause and tentative question which followed. 'I didn't know that was still going. Or am I thinking of something else? Didn't *Firing Line* do a piece on them a while back?'

'That's absolutely right,' said Morgan, and stopped. She tried again.

'That's absolutely right, and I was the one—' She found that she was trembling slightly. 'I was the one who—' She hadn't realised that it was possible to be literally speechless with rage, but she simply could not force her tongue to articulate another word.

'That's what I thought.' The dark face was impassive. 'I can't do this without you—I know that even if your trustees don't—and if you can't do your part I'd rather know now. I don't want to go to the trouble of getting you the ear of someone with a lot of money if you're going to be choked up by all the things you'd like to say about me but can't. One look at your face and he'd smell a rat.'

He raised an eyebrow. 'If you can get it out of your system by calling me names, go right ahead. Otherwise let's call it off before I waste any more of my time.'

Morgan bit back the retort which sprang to her lips. 'It's been a bit sudden,' she said stiffly. 'I'll manage.'

'Really?' The grey eyes were sceptical. 'I'm not convinced by anything I've seen so far. Who's doing the teaching now that you're holed up with the books?'

'We've got a couple of volunteers,' Morgan said faintly, trying not to think of the chaotic classrooms she'd seen on her occasional visits. 'Bob couldn't stay with things so uncertain, and, of course, it's better not to have people drawing salaries—'

'Volunteers? Are they properly trained teachers? It is a *school*, isn't it, not just a day-care centre?'

She realised abruptly that he'd shifted back to the inquisitorial stranger. 'Well, they're not trained teachers, but at least it means the children have some continuity—'

'Oh, for God's sake!' Richard broke across this in disgust. 'Morgan, you're not answering the voice of conscience, you're trying to persuade someone that this is an organisation that's genuinely helping children who need it. You sound as if you're trying to get *me* to reassure *you* that it's a good thing. Quite frankly— speaking as PR consultant rather than hypothetical millionaire—you make my hair stand on end. Do you mean that there are no proper teachers now that you're out of the classroom?'

'No. I mean, yes, that is what I mean,' Morgan said wearily. 'Just because the trustees have stumped up twenty thousand pounds for you doesn't mean they'd fund a teacher's salary. How can I recruit teachers I can't pay? So what *can* I say if somebody asks me who's doing the teaching?'

'You tell them you're actively recruiting three teachers who specialise in the school's demanding type of class,' Richard said calmly. 'And it had better be the truth, or I'll be gone so fast that you won't see me for dust. I'm prepared to put my name on the line for the kind of classroom I saw you running, not for a zoo run by well-meaning amateurs.'

'And suppose someone says they thought all the money was gone?' Morgan asked sarcastically. 'Do I say I'm actively looking for that too?'

'You say that now that Ruth's gone a lot more money can go directly to the classroom, and the aim is to raise a hundred thousand pounds by the start of the new school term. And you needn't look shifty or shamefaced about it; that is my aim, and provided you work with me rather than against me there's no reason why I shouldn't get it. There was a quiet confidence in his voice that was more convincing than boastfulness would have been.

'That's *if* you work with me. You've got to be ready for tough questions, Morgan, not hope people won't ask them.' The grey eyes raked over her mercilessly. 'You have a very expressive face, and a habit of sharing your doubts with anyone who challenges you; I don't want to see you look at people the way I've seen you look at me, daring them to press the point.'

'I thought my honesty was what you particularly liked,' Morgan flashed out angrily.

If she'd expected to disconcert him she was disappointed. The brilliant eyes widened in ironic surprise. 'Someone I didn't expect what I liked to be very high on your list of priorities,' he said drily. 'I've seen you wear things that I personally found more appealing than what you've got on now; that doesn't mean I'd advise you to wear a wet T-shirt to a business meeting. Do you want me to explain why?'

Morgan shook her head. His words had reminded

her abruptly of that weekend, only a couple of months or so ago, when she'd promised Elaine to behave conventionally; no need to press home the point that her inept attempts at concealment had had serious consequences. She'd been a teacher then—a good one—and now she was an overworked administrator.

Just for a minute she'd felt a warm glow when he'd praised her teaching. But the whole drift of his speech confirmed what experience had shown her anyway: it wasn't enough to be good at that. It wasn't even enough to be good at business unless you looked and talked the part.

She frowned, staring at the lovely Oriental rug beneath her feet, the priceless silver and crystal on the sideboard. They seemed to say to her, We belong to rich, silly Brenda Vavasour, who can't read a spread-sheet and can't tell a good classroom from a bad one but who can tell the difference between an Armani and a high-street copy. Richard can persuade someone like that to give him twenty thousand pounds to play with. What are *you* going to say?

She shook herself and raised her head proudly, meeting Richard's eyes. 'That's absolutely right!' she said in a strong, ringing tone of voice. 'In fact I was the one who got Richard Kavanagh interested in the char-ity. And now that the director's gone Richard's spear-heading a campaign to raise funds for the school.' Her warm, husky voice lingered with a hint of intimacy, a shade of grateful admiration, on the name.

'It was doing good work all along—of course Richard spotted that from the start—but that's nothing com-pared to what we can do now that funds aren't being siphoned off to administration. If it interests you I hope you'll come down for a visit—but even if you can't manage that I do hope you'll come to our reception at the House of Commons in the autumn.'

She paused, the glowing look instantly quenched. 'How was that?' she asked.

'Spot on,' said Richard. 'I think I've created a monster.'

'You're the monster, Richard,' said Morgan drily. 'Or do you only like honesty some of the time?'

His jaw hardened. 'At the moment there's not much to choose between your honesty and your acting.' He paused, then added grimly, 'But by the time I'm finished you'll mean every word of that little speech.'

CHAPTER TEN

KAVANAGH'S KIDS. It jumped out at Morgan from the cover—the *cover*, no less—of her Sunday supplement, emblazoned across a picture of Richard looking debonair and the children looking excited.

Morgan poured herself a cup of coffee and opened the magazine, scowling.

She hadn't had a chance to look at the Sunday papers on Sunday, of course—she'd been at the office all day, snatching a few precious hours when Richard wasn't around to think of something he needed done instantly. But now, at eight o'clock on Monday morning, after three hours of working, glassy-eyed, through correspondence, she'd decided to take a break. Richard wouldn't be in for another hour.

There was no doubt about it—it was a master-stroke. There was a profile of Richard inside, making high-minded remarks about responsible journalism and about how sometimes it wasn't enough just to report abuses. And because the piece had come out a month after his arrival there were tangible results to show for his presence—two vans sponsored by a manufacturer, two extremely competent teachers who'd taken not only the children but also the volunteers in hand. . .

Morgan grimaced, thinking of the argument she'd had with Richard over their recruitment, or rather over the week it had taken her to get things moving. That was when things had really started to go wrong. . .

By the end of Richard's first week in the office Morgan had looked back to her weeks pre-Richard as a halcyon period when she'd had time for her own work. The word 'prioritise' was constantly on Richard's

lips; what it meant, she'd discovered, was 'Drop everything and do what I say instantly'.

She'd spent that first week in a strange mood,
alternating between furious resentment at his dictato-
rial ways, the impossibility of getting any of her own,
equally vital work done, and excitement at seeing
projects started that, if she could only keep up with
him, would undoubtedly pay off. Sometimes the sheer
hard work dissolved her resentment; sometimes it left
her fretting anxiously about everything she'd been
forced to leave undone.

On the Thursday they'd gone out, as they had every
night that week, and Morgan had trotted out the lines
that Richard had given her, which had become so
familiar that they were automatic.

'So you're not actually in the classroom yourself
these days?' Sir Michael, head of one of the largest
private banks in the country, had been sympathetic,
and Morgan had responded, talking wistfully of how
long it had been since she'd been able to work with the
children herself.

Afterwards Richard was scathing.

'Dry up, darling?' he asked sarcastically. 'Forget your
lines?'

'I don't know what you're talking about,' Morgan
said resentfully.

'Whatever happened to actively seeking the best
teachers for a demanding class? Or did that just slip
your mind?'

'He was *interested*!' Morgan protested.

'For God's sake, Morgan,' he said impatiently.
'That's one of the oldest tricks in the book. You tell
someone such and such must be very difficult, and look
sympathetic, and they're eating out of your hand.'

'I'm sure it is one of your tricks, Richard,' Morgan
said acidly. 'But some people really do help someone

they like even if they *haven't* got all the answers. Of course I don't expect you to understand that.'

'Unlike dear, sympathetic Sir Michael,' Richard said caustically. 'Come off it, Morgan. You must realise it wasn't a very good idea; don't take out your bad temper on me just because I had the bad taste to point it out.' He pulled up in front of Morgan's house and cut the engine. 'Speaking of teachers, by the way, how are you getting on with recruiting? Any nibbles?'

Morgan thought briefly of four days eaten up as Richard had set her combing through files, donor-base, social services literature, spirited her away to a Chelsea designer to 'do something about her clothes', dragged her to one party after another. 'I haven't had time to do anything about it,' she said pointedly.

'I see.' The temperature in the car dropped about twenty degrees. 'So in fact you're *not* actively searching for competent staff.' The slow voice was deadly. 'It's more of a hobby. Something you do in your spare time, like stamp collecting.'

Morgan had seen that cold irony deployed to devastating effect on *Firing Line* on flagrant examples of inefficiency. She was having none of it.

'Don't you dare take that tone with me, Richard,' she rapped back. 'From the minute you walked in the door on Monday you've done nothing but ask questions you need the answers to instantly, can't wait, top priority, drop everything.'

'You've got to be able to prioritise, Morgan—'

It was the last straw. '*Prioritise!*' shouted Morgan. 'What do you mean by prioritise, Richard—me first? I can't even write a cheque without your approval—so don't blame *me* for doing what you insisted couldn't wait.'

'I haven't been literally standing at your shoulder,' he pointed out. 'If you'd placed the ads and written out a couple of personal cheques and presented me with a

fait accompli, you can't really think I'd have walked
out or refused to approve your claim for expenses.'

'No,' Morgan said grudgingly.

'So it sounds to me as though you knew what needed
to be done and didn't do it just so you could blame me
later when things went wrong,' he said coolly. 'Well, I
hope that gives you some satisfaction, but it hasn't
done the children a hell of a lot of good. In future it
might be better if you thought about the children,
instead of following my instructions to the letter.'

And naïve, gullible Morgan had actually felt guilty
and wondered whether he was right. Perhaps she *was*
nursing her resentment. Perhaps they *could* work
together as a team. Perhaps she could even explain
how much she had to do. . . But that was before she'd
realised just how calculating Richard could be when he
wanted to get his way.

Morgan leafed through the Sunday supplement article with a rather bitter smile, remembering her shamefaced apologies, the way she'd rushed into the office to
write the adverts first thing the next morning. It had
been the morning when Richard had publicly launched
his campaign for A Child's Place, with a stunt reminiscent of the early, flamboyant days of *Firing Line*.

He'd abseiled off the Telecom Tower with a child
strapped to his back.

Morgan hadn't been able to see this at first hand, for
the simple reason that there had had to be *somebody*
at the office. But she'd caught it on the radio, and later,
again and again, on the evening news—the moment
when he'd reached the ground, and a chorus of journalists had bayed, 'Isn't it irresponsible of you to risk a
child's life?'

'I don't play games with the lives of children.' On
television you'd got the full force of the Kavanagh
pause as the electric eyes had gazed straight into the
camera. 'Can you say the same? After all,' he'd said

sardonically, 'the children on the streets and in hostels and in bed and breakfasts aren't made of plastic.' And then he'd pointedly unstrapped a dummy from his back.

All very fine, Morgan reminded herself now, if you conveniently forgot how this all started in the first place—but her heart wasn't in it. She suspected that she was really only jealous—she would have *loved* to abseil off the Telecom Tower, but no one was interested in Morgan Roberts. Richard Kavanagh was another matter. Of course the phone had rung off the hook.

One of the callers had been Elaine.

And it had been then that the whole nasty pattern had fallen into place.

'You've really got to hand it to Richard,' Elaine said offhandedly. 'As an exercise in damage limitation it takes some beating.'

'Yes, it's marvellous, isn't it?' said Morgan. 'The phones haven't stopped ringing all morning.'

Elaine laughed out loud at this piece of naïvety. With just a touch of condescension she set her innocent elder sister straight: Morgan hadn't been the only one outraged by the programme on A Child's Place, and there'd been an enormous postbag of letters from indignant viewers. Richard just wanted to improve his image.

'But surely he must be used to offending people by now?' Morgan protested.

Elaine hesitated. 'Put it this way,' she said at last. 'I *hope* that's why he's doing it. Because otherwise. . .'

'Yes?'

'Otherwise I don't like to think of what he's up to,' the younger girl said bluntly. 'I don't think you understand what it's like for a man like Richard to be rejected by a woman, Morgan. I heard about all the things you told him after that programme. . . If he *isn't* trying to mend his image, he may be trying to get back at you one way or another.'

Fear clutched Morgan's heart. 'By sabotaging the charity?' she asked.

'Or getting you to fall for him—'

'There's no danger of *that*!' Morgan said sourly.

Elaine chuckled. 'Glad to hear it. I know it sounds pretty melodramatic, which is why I think it's *probably* sheer pragmatism at work. But be on your guard, will you? He's a dangerous man to cross, for all that spectacular charm.'

'Charm?' spluttered Morgan. '*Charm*! The man's a *snake*!' And she slammed down the receiver.

She dismissed after only a moment's unease Elaine's talk of revenge—but the point about his image was frighteningly plausible. And the worst of it was that Richard was shamelessly taking up huge amounts of her own working time to promote spectacular, high-profile activity—things that would make everyone *see* how much he was doing for the charity—while obstructing the unglamorous unravelling of Ruth's legacy, which was crucial to the school's survival. But there was nothing she could do; if she refused to co-operate with him, the trustees would simply put someone else in her place.

He came in halfway through the afternoon, the reckless face split by a grin which combined self-satisfaction and hilarity in about equal measures. 'Did you catch the landing?' he asked, perching on her desk, the brilliant eyes throwing off sparks of amusement. '"Isn't it irresponsible of you to risk a child's life?"' he mimicked, and laughed out loud. 'What a scream. Many calls?'

'Lots,' Morgan said tightly. 'Congratulations,' she added politely. 'It was very spectacular.' And she pushed two cheques across the desk for him to sign, with a brisk movement that put an end to a dull subject.

A black eyebrow shot up at this snub. 'You don't fool me,' he told her mockingly, scrawling a bold signature across the cheques. 'You're just jealous because you'd have liked to do it yourself.' He tossed the cheques back, mouth twitching. 'Well, if you're very nice to me maybe I'll take you next time instead of Sadie. I gave her a kiss afterwards but it didn't do too much for her; something tells me I'm just not her type.'

'Isn't she yours, though?' Morgan asked sweetly. 'At least she can't talk back. "I don't play games with the lives of children,"' she mimicked sarcastically. 'Well, a woman with a mind of her own might wonder just exactly what you *were* doing on *Firing Line* that night.'

The amusement vanished from his face. 'Might she, Morgan?' he asked drily. 'Wish you'd been there to prick the bubble? Well, you can wonder what you damn well like in that suspicious mind of yours, but if you ever say anything like that in public when I'm trying to sell the place I'll—'

'What?' Morgan asked scornfully. 'Give me a rough kiss?'

'It's not a game, Morgan,' he said coldly. 'The day you interfere with me is the last day you work here.'

From then on their relationship had deteriorated steadily.

If they went out for an evening Richard analysed her performance afterwards as if she'd been auditioning for *Firing Line*, criticising her appearance, dissecting what he'd heard of her conversation, grilling her on people she'd talked to, what she'd said to them, when he wasn't there. If she worked in the office there was always a mountain of work to be tackled—sometimes she thought that he was daring her to object, to give him an excuse to get rid of her.

What he'd taught her, Morgan now thought grittily, was that you could go on indefinitely with three hours' sleep a night. She did her own work after cocktail parties, or before nine a.m., or at weekends. And when people said how wonderful it was of Richard to drop everything and give all his time to the charity she smiled and said it was absolutely wonderful.

They'd used one of the stills from the Telecom Tower descent in the Sunday supplement, she saw, but there were plenty of others with real children. He'd been lucky in his photographer, Morgan thought sourly, looking at a series of charming 'candid' shots. Richard probably wasn't capable of looking bad in a photograph—but the *Firing Line* audience wouldn't have seen him with that laughing, open expression. A million female viewers would be suffering withdrawal symptoms and sending in their cheques. Nobody looking at those pictures would guess that he was cold, heartless, calculating...

Nine o'clock. Morgan drank the last of her cold coffee and reached for the phone. Hexham & Horsham Notions & Novelties should be open now; it was time to cancel, if she still could, the order for five thousand toiletry bags which she'd discovered only last night at the back of another of Ruth's chaotic files.

The phone rang as her hand closed on the receiver—an enquiry in response to the article. She jotted down details of the person's address, and as she hung up heard the now familiar sound of long legs coming up the stairs three at a time.

As always she tensed when they reached the top landing, and tensed again as her own door swung open.

And as always, no matter how often she prepared herself for it, there was the same shock of seeing him enter a room.

'Congratulations,' she told him curtly, nodding at the magazine. 'Everything's going to plan, I see.'

'Well, I didn't bargain for—' He laughed as the phone rang again and he picked it up. 'A Child's

Place. . .yes. . .oh, I think we have a few tickets left.'
He winked at Morgan and began scribbling details on
a pad. 'Wonderful; we'll look forward to seeing you on
the night.' He put down the receiver. 'Sally was an
angel to do it.'

'Well, I expect you asked her nicely,' Morgan said
sweetly.

A black eyebrow shot up. 'Jealous?'

'Don't make me laugh.'

'I don't waste time on the impossible,' he said
angrily. 'What the hell is the matter this time, Morgan?'

'I'm sorry, did I miss my cue?' she shot back. 'My
hero!' she breathed soulfully.

'Have I missed something?' he demanded, his grey
eyes crackling. 'Am I imagining things, or has something about this article incurred your displeasure?'

'Why, Richard,' she protested. 'It's absolutely
delightful. I'm sure it will do your image no *end* of
good.'

'My *image*?' He stared at her in astonishment. 'I
don't give a *damn* about my image!' he shouted. 'Can't
you get that into your head?' He brought a fist down
on Ruth's desk and cursed as papers cascaded to the
floor. 'Morgan, I don't know where you got this insane
idea from, but will you, for God's sake, give it a rest? I
don't lie awake nights worrying about whether people
know I'm nice to children and animals.'

The phone rang. 'A Child's Place!' he snarled. 'Yes,
we'll send you details.' He wrote something down and
banged down the receiver.

'And if I did worry about it,' he added caustically, 'I
wouldn't have chosen this as a way to look appealing;
I'd have opened a bloody hedgehog sanctuary, which
would have been a damn sight less prickly than you.'

He stalked out of the room and slammed the door,
leaving more papers to slide to the floor.

An hour later he was back.

'We've had a real piece of luck,' he told her. 'Someone's backed out of *Ten to Ten* at the last minute, and Brian says if I don't mind coming at short notice the spot's mine.'

'Wonderful,' said Morgan tepidly.

Richard sat on the edge of her desk, swinging one leg. He raised an eyebrow. 'Well, it may be,' he said. 'But he won't be doing me any favours, you know. He'll be looking for a weak spot, and if he finds one he'll make the most of it.'

'Well, good luck,' said Morgan.

'I'll need a bit more than that,' he said curtly. 'The first thing he'll go for is the question of whether we're reaching the children that most need help. In other words, what kind of liaison do we have with other organisations for the homeless. . .?'

'Well, we don't really have any,' Morgan pointed out. 'We've sent them our literature, of course—'

'That was nice of us,' he said sarcastically.

'But we didn't have funds for a salary for someone to deal with that,' she continued patiently. 'All we had was teachers, Ruth, and Ruth's secretary—'

'I know all that.' He cut her off abruptly. 'What I want is information on how we *could* fit in with the other work being done. It's one thing to know your limitations, but quite another not even to aim at doing your job properly.' He tossed a sheet of paper across the desk. 'I'll be out most of the day seeing people, but I think this list covers everything. I'll be back at about four, so that should give you plenty of time.'

Morgan began to point out that she had work of her own to do—but Richard was already out the door.

She sighed and picked up the sheet of paper. She knew the answers to a few of Richard's questions off the top of her head and scribbled them in the margin. But the others would require real research, perhaps a whole day's work.

She scowled. Couldn't Richard just for once do his own research? And did he really need to know all this? In a perfect world he might want to have all the answers in minute detail—but, after all, he'd told her to prioritise. He'd even told her that if she thought something was right she should present him with a *fait accompli*. Well, she would take care of *her* top priorities, and then spend an hour or two after lunch on Richard's little list.

Morgan worked solidly through to two o'clock, and then decided that she'd better start on Richard's questions.

She made calls to several other charities that worked with the homeless. It was a little more complicated than she'd imagined—one of the people she needed to talk to had been in that morning, but was now out of the office, and the person who'd answered the phone wasn't very helpful. But she persevered, and managed to fill a couple of sheets of paper with notes.

At four Richard returned, looking rather weary. He took the pages of notes which Morgan handed him and began to turn away, reading as he went. He'd hardly reached the door, however, before he turned back and looked up again. 'Is this all there is?' he asked. 'It's pretty scrappy.'

'I'm afraid it's all I had time for,' said Morgan.

He stared at her. 'Are you serious?' he asked incredulously.

'I had a lot of other things to do.'

'This is a chance in a million—what could possibly be more important than—?' He glanced abruptly down at his watch. 'Well, there's no point in wasting time arguing,' he said grimly. 'We've a few hours to work with.'

By the time Richard set off for the studio Morgan had discovered just how much research could be crammed into a few short hours. Richard had been

solidly on the phone; Morgan had been buried in the
charity's substantial collection of literature on law and
the social services. When she'd handed him the results
of her work, however, he'd taken them unsmilingly.
'Thanks,' he'd said coolly. 'Maybe tomorrow you can
explain to me just what it was that couldn't wait.'

Watching him on television at home that night,
Morgan was relieved to see that Richard seemed
unfazed by the probing questions; he readily admitted
to the difficulties faced by the charity, but managed to
make it sound so much like a gallant underdog that she
couldn't imagine anyone being put off by them. And
he was surprisingly moving on the subject of the
children, without any of the cloying sentimentality that
Ruth had always brought to the theme.

For a moment even Morgan almost thought that he
genuinely cared about them rather than about his own
dented image—but then she remembered who she had
to deal with. No, he didn't care about anyone but
himself, but, to give the devil his due, he was giving the
performance of his life.

Next morning, forcing out the praise that this bravura
called for, Morgan was cut ruthlessly short.

'Don't you *ever* do that to me again.'

Richard began pacing up and down the office,
favouring her with a number of unprintable comments
on the interview and the wanton irresponsibility that
had left him improperly briefed. 'If you can't do
something I ask you to do, don't you *ever* let me go off
thinking it's taken care of,' he concluded wrathfully.
'Tell me so I can make other arrangements.'

This from the man who never took no for an answer.
'*What* other arrangements?' asked Morgan. 'Arrangements to browbeat me into doing what you want?'

Richard didn't smile. 'Well, in this particular case
you're damn right. What on earth were you doing—?

No, I don't even want to know what you thought had a better claim on your time; if I did I'd probably wring your neck. For God's sake, Morgan, this was a chance to reach millions of people; if something like that comes along you grab it with both hands and give it your best shot.'

'I don't know what you're complaining about,' Morgan defended herself. 'You spent most of the time talking about yourself anyway. You don't need me to spend all day researching just so you can tell anec-dotes—'

She quailed before the cold fury in his eyes.

'*Quite*.' The word was like the flick of a whip.

'Richard—' Morgan met his eyes straight on '—what do you think of this?' She picked up a toiletry bag in the shape of a child's head and threw it none too politely across the room.

'What the hell is it?' he asked impatiently.

'It's a toiletry bag,' Morgan informed him wearily. 'Specially commissioned by Ruth. Which the manufac-turers never got round to producing when we were broke and nobody had heard of us. But now. . .' She paused and glared at him. 'Now that we're famous they tell me they're just starting a production run of five thousand, and I've had to talk to five separate people to get them to even consider letting us cancel the order.'

'And?'

'They're considering it.' Morgan folded her arms on her desk and looked at him steadily. 'The point is,' she said, 'it's twelve thousand pounds. Well, I know as well as you do that you can't get the kind of TV coverage you got last night for twelve thousand pounds; maybe you could argue it would be worth sacrificing the money to make sure you had all the answers.'

It took about two seconds to sink in. 'And then have

word get out that the loony marketing scheme is alive and well. . .? *Hell*,' he said with feeling.

There were some people, Morgan reflected, who wouldn't recognise that for an apology.

He ran a hand through his hair irritably. 'Any more of these on the horizon?'

'Not that I know of.'

'Thank God for that.' He shrugged. 'Well, as long as you're here there's a couple of things—' he began.

Didn't he ever learn? 'I am *not* here,' Morgan said firmly.

'What?'

'I am not here!' repeated Morgan. 'I am *not here* to do your "couple of things". If they're that important, *you* do them. If you need to find something in the files, *you* look for it. If you want to find out something about the donor-base, *you* work it out. *I am not here.*'

'In words of one syllable,' said Richard. 'Great.' He left the room, slamming the door behind him.

I don't care, thought Morgan. She gritted her teeth and began to work down through the pile marked 'urgent'.

It was only after she'd drafted a couple of letters that something odd struck her. Why *was* Richard so angry? If all he cared about was his own image, why should he care whether he'd had to steer clear of certain topics concerning the charity? He'd carried off the interview with his usual panache—the whole exercise had polished up Richard's image until it sparkled. But if he *didn't* just care about his image that meant it *hadn't* been just an act; he'd *meant* those things he'd said about the children.

Was it possible that she'd misjudged him?

She was in a doubtful, uncertain mood when she saw him again, at just after four.

'What are you doing tonight?' he asked her, leaning against the doorjamb.

Morgan looked up from a reassuringly depleted 'urgent' tray. 'Are you actually *asking* me?'

'I wondered whether you'd like to come round to my place,' he stunned her by saying. 'I thought I'd have a look at Elaine's latest solo flight—I taped it since we had to be out and about on Friday. Care to join me?'

Morgan hesitated. She was tempted to accept this overture—but after the weeks of criticism the last thing she felt in the mood for was an evening of listening to Richard rave about Elaine. 'I'm not sure,' she temporised.

To her surprise Richard gave her a suddenly searching look. 'You caught the first one?'

Elaine had made mincemeat of a self-improvement guru. 'I don't think he was a charlatan, just naïve,' Morgan said noncommittally.

'Mmm, she was a bit heavy-handed. We'd deliberately picked someone who was a bit of a joke to ease her into the show, and when she savaged him. . .' He shrugged. 'Well, it takes time to hit your stride.' A sardonic eyebrow swooped up towards his hairline. 'But I suppose you think it's exactly what I did all the time!' he added accusingly. 'After all, I eat babies for breakfast, don't I?'

'Don't be ridiculous,' Morgan said uncomfortably. She couldn't quite pinpoint the difference—after all, Richard could be merciless in his line of questioning. But he'd never seemed *spiteful*. . .

'Oh, no, that's right, it would be bad for my image,' he agreed sardonically.

Morgan thrust her hands in her pockets. Her chin jutted out. 'Elaine was probably nervous,' she said. 'It's new to her. But when you did that piece on A Child's Place you knew *exactly* what you were doing. Of course you didn't look spiteful or malicious—you're too clever for that.' Her smoky eyes met his directly. 'But you *did* humiliate Ruth publicly. If you really cared about the children, why didn't you come to me first?'

Richard ran his hands through his hair. 'You think I should have gone to the trustees and said, Your director's a crook, but, don't worry, you can hand it all over to Huckleberry Finn? How the hell was I supposed to know you had a business machine for a brain?'

'Well, you had plenty of time to find out if you'd cared,' retorted Morgan. 'But then it wasn't my *mind* you were interested in, was it?'

Richard's eyes began to sparkle with temper. 'Morgan, for God's sake—' He threw himself away from her and began to stalk up and down the room. At last he came back and gripped her shoulders. 'Will you listen to me?' he demanded exasperatedly. 'You can't seriously think I lost interest in you because you didn't jump into bed with me?'

Morgan raised an eyebrow. 'Oh, no?' she said ironically, and winced as his grip tightened on her arms.

'How could I go on seeing you, platonically or otherwise, with this thing starting to unravel?'

'Of course you couldn't,' Morgan agreed sympathetically. 'Who knows what you might have let drop? And of course it would have gone *straight* to Ruth—'

'The thought did cross my mind,' he said coolly.

'*What*?'

'You obviously knew *something* was wrong.' His eyes were like burnished steel. 'From the moment we met— met *properly*—' he gave a wolfish grin '—if that's the word for it—you had "guilty conscience" written all over you.'

'You thought I *knew* about Ruth?' Morgan tried to struggle free from his grasp.

He looked at her gravely. 'It was a possibility. And frankly, if you did, I wanted nothing to do with you. And if you didn't—well, as far as I'm concerned, the one bright spot in the whole sorry mess is that we *didn't* start an affair before I'd realised what a can of worms the place was.' He stared down at her, fixing her with the full force of that charismatic gaze.

Could it be true? Morgan could feel her heart start to thump heavily in her chest as she gazed, mesmerised, into his eyes. He hadn't known about her business background; she had acted suspiciously; maybe Richard had been trying to act with integrity. Maybe he still was.

'He can sound fair-minded and impartial when it suits him, which is usually when he wants to get someone into bed. . .'

She heard the words so clearly that she might have had Elaine whispering over her shoulder. Once she'd dismissed them as ridiculous—but then, she thought bitterly, she'd once thought that she could trust her intuitions about Richard. Well, there was one way to find out.

Morgan lowered her eyes. 'So does that mean,' she said huskily, looking up at him, her smoky eyes wide, 'that we could start an affair now that we're on the same side?'

She knew the answer before he spoke. His hands loosened on her arms, and a faint smile curved the sensuous mouth as he bent his head. 'Morgan. . .' he murmured.

'I know you took it for granted,' she said softly, 'that we couldn't be personally involved—'

'Changed my mind.'

'Changed your mind?' There was a hint of laughter in the husky voice.

'All right,' he conceded. 'I lied.' The old infectious smile lit his eyes, but Morgan felt no temptation to respond.

'I'm so glad to be appreciated for my mind,' she said acidly, jerking free from him.

He stared at her; instead of having the decency to

look ashamed at being caught out he actually looked angry.

'Would you mind explaining what that was all about?' he asked. 'What's the matter? Was I supposed to go off the idea once I found you could read a spreadsheet?'

'You know perfectly well what the matter is!' snapped Morgan. 'Why can't you tell the truth for once? All you want is to improve your image, and you thought you might as well have a little recreation on the side, so now you think you've got to bamboozle me into thinking—'

'Why don't *I* tell the truth?' Richard cut across her without compunction. He glared at her. 'You wouldn't recognise the truth if you fell over it. I don't know why I bother.' The electric eyes gazed down at her, taking in her defiant, accusing look, and a rather wry smile tugged at his mouth. 'Well, you must trust me a little, Morgan. What makes you think I won't walk out now I know I can't have my wicked way with you?'

Morgan didn't hesitate for an instant. 'The only reason you're here anyway is to improve your image,' she said crisply. 'I can't believe a little thing like this will put you off.'

'Will you *forget* about my *image*?'

Morgan hugged herself in satisfaction—suave, imperturbable Richard was actually shouting. She'd obviously touched a sore point.

'I'm not ready to eat my words yet, Richard,' she said sweetly.

'You will,' he said. 'I'll see you do it if it's the last thing I do.'

CHAPTER ELEVEN

KAVANAGH TO THE RESCUE!

Morgan picked up the first of the stack of tabloids on her desk and wondered whether she'd gone too far.

When morning star Elaine Roberts joned TV heart-throb Richard Kavanagh on the news show *Firing Line*, rumour had it TV's most eligible bachelor had fallen at last.

Morgan winced. And yet it had seemed such a good idea at the time—a way of giving Richard a taste of his own medicine. . . So all he cared about was the children, was it? He didn't give a damn about his image? Well, if anyone was going to eat their words it wasn't going to be her.

She'd gone to yet another grand reception where everyone had seen *Ten to Ten* and had had to tell her how wonderful it was. Wonderful, wonderful, wonderful, Morgan had agreed, gritting her teeth, and afterwards could never remember just when it had become obvious that everyone thought there was a personal angle. The only question in anybody's mind had been whether she was sleeping with Richard *yet*.

And the next day she'd started getting calls from journalists asking for the inside story on the 'romance'.

She'd been about to reject this out of hand when a voice had spoken in her ear—a sarcastic, drawling, arrogant, all-knowing voice.

'Don't think about what I'd like, think what would be good for the charity. . . Present me with a *fait accompli*. . . Learn to prioritise. . . You can't throw away a chance to reach millions of possible supporters...'

All right, Mr Know It All, she'd thought suddenly. You *asked* for it...

Richard Kavanagh—what he was really like. Well, they wouldn't find that out from her—they wanted the superhero, the heartthrob, the sex symbol, and by God they were going to get him.

Now! readers voted Elaine 'TV personality you'd most like to wake up in bed with' in a recent survey, whilst Richard has come top of the table as TV's sexiest newsman for the past five years.

A match made in heaven?

It seems Richard had other ideas, and Elaine's sister Morgan, a stunningly attractive brunette, has stolen a march on the blonde bombshell.

For the past month female viewers have watched the screen in vain for their favourite face. Richard, we can now reveal, has been working one-to-one with Morgan in a tiny school for homeless children in London's East End.

Morgan had deliberately timed her interviews to come out on the day of the long-awaited jazz evening. Gleefully she'd imagined Richard circulating among the curious, trying to look unconcerned, just as she'd had to do for so many weeks. Now, looking at the clichés she'd piled on with a trowel, she began to imagine just what Richard's reaction was likely to be to this little joke. Maybe it hadn't been such a good idea after all...

Asked whether personal feelings had played a part in Richard's decision to help the charity, the slim twenty-six-year-old replied, 'Richard is an intensely private person. We've never discussed his motives,

but I know he was very impressed by how much the
school means to the children.'

Asked how she found working with Richard, a
notorious womaniser, Morgan admitted that he was
'very attractive' but insisted, 'Our relationship is
purely professional.' But a mischievous smile suggested she could say more—if only she would!

That was the *Daily Post*. The *Sentinel* didn't bother
to be coy. A full two-page spread in the centre of the
paper showed a picture of Richard surrounded by
pictures of famous former girlfriends—including
Elaine.

A line of hearts led to a picture of Morgan in the
lower right-hand corner, with the caption 'AND THE
WINNER IS...'

The *Semaphore* had played up the knight-in-shining-
armour theme, and presented Richard as undergoing
trials to win the hand of a lady. 'How long will she hold
out?' it demanded. 'Mr Love 'em and Leave 'em meets
his match'. The *Messenger* dwelt with relish on the
theme of 'the harder they fall', extracting every last
humiliating implication from Morgan's refusal to admit
outright that she was in love with Richard.

And every single paper lingered in fascination on the
qualities of the woman who'd managed to ensnare
Richard; in one she had a 'haunting, indefinable
beauty', in another 'gamine charm', in a third 'a
strange, fey quality'. She'd never realised before that
journalists just invented things to suit themselves.

At last Morgan put the papers aside and forced
herself to tackle some of the work on her desk. It was
hard to concentrate, for she found that she was listening, in spite of herself, for footsteps on the stairs, but
she managed somehow to deal with a number of items.
At about five-thirty she heard the street door slam.

Footsteps came up the stairs and retreated into the

room across the landing. She was, she realised, shirking the inevitable; impatiently she stood up, gathered up the papers and went into the other office.

Richard was standing by his desk, leafing through a report. He looked up when she came in. 'Any new developments?' he asked casually.

'I gave some interviews to some journalists while you were away,' said Morgan.

'Oh, yes? Any good?'

'You'd better have a look at these,' Morgan said reluctantly. A look of faint surprise greeted the sheaf of tabloids she handed over. He propped one hand on the desk and began looking over the first one; there was a terrible silence while he opened it and turned to the inside spread. For several minutes the only sound was the faint whisper of pages being turned as he worked his way down the pile.

At long last he looked up.

Morgan realised that she had had a faint hope that he would treat the whole thing as a joke, but there was not the slightest trace of amusement in the eyes that met hers. 'Congratulations,' he said. 'You must have enjoyed yourself.'

'You did tell me to think of A Child's Place first, rather than about what you like,' Morgan said awkwardly. 'I know you probably don't care for it much.'

'I said I thought you'd enjoyed yourself,' he said coolly. 'You knew damned well what I'd think of this, but you'd the perfect excuse to go ahead and say I'd as good as told you to do it.'

'Well, I—I suppose you must be used to this kind of thing by now...' Morgan faltered. She found it surprisingly difficult to meet his eyes—if only she *could* enjoy her revenge. She tried to think of all the sarcastic things she'd wanted to say. I thought you didn't care about your image, she'd wanted to taunt him. 'You must have had a few exes telling all before this.'

'No,' said Richard. 'As a matter of fact, you're the first.'

Morgan swallowed. 'Well, at least it's in a good cause,' she said. 'Or do you think—do you think it's the wrong sort of publicity to do any good?'

'No,' Richard said again. 'It's very good publicity.'

'You could issue a denial,' said Morgan.

'I could,' said Richard, his eyes like steel. 'But I think I'd rather give them something to talk about.'

There was an odd note in his voice that Morgan did not like at all. 'What do you mean?' she managed.

'You seem to have done a pretty good job of making people think I'm here because I've fallen for you, and that you're not having any,' he said drily. 'Problem is, they can't keep running that. So let's give them something to be going on with.'

'Wh-what—?' Morgan stammered.

'They'll all be there tonight. Well, time to look like you're starting to fall, darling. Stick to me; follow me with your eyes if we're separated; don't dance with anyone else—'

'Why don't we just announce our engagement?' Morgan said sarcastically.

'What, and spoil the suspense?' His eyes widened in astonishment. 'I'm shocked. No, we'll keep them guessing. I dare say we can manage a goodnight kiss to keep them happy—'

'I can hardly wait.'

'Well, he said slowly, 'if you want one to be going on with. . .' He raised a hand to her jaw. Eyes white-hot with anger blazed into hers. 'Do you want a practice session, Morgan?'

Her heart was pounding in her chest. 'N-no.'

His hand fell abruptly. 'Something to look forward to, then.'

*   *   *

Afterwards Morgan always remembered with disbelief that the evening was actually a success. Tickets for the raffle sold briskly, the celebrities who had promised to come came and stood to be photographed, a number of guests even made donations on top of the price of their tickets. There was even a loyal crowd from Richard's old studio. From time to time it occurred to Morgan that the band seemed to be playing quite well too. And a throng of reporters had shown up, sure enough, keen to get down a blow-by-blow account of the hottest romance in town.

For the first hour they circulated among the guests, Richard occasionally drawing Morgan casually but firmly after him when she seemed about to be separated by the crowd. He did nothing so obvious as stand arm in arm with her, but from time to time he would place an arm round her shoulder, or bend down as if to make an intimate remark—it was usually 'Smile!'—and every time there was an explosion of flashbulbs.

After a while Morgan forgot about everything except her weary feet; certainly she forgot about Richard's threat to dance with her. Until, that was, Delia Jervis got up to sing.

Miss Jervis insisted that she didn't want everyone sitting around on their hands as if it were some damned opera; she wanted people to dance. The band began playing the introduction to 'Someone to Watch Over Me'. And the audience sat at its tables, waiting for someone else to go first.

Miss Jervis waited, unhurried, by her microphone.

The band did a reprise of the introduction to 'Someone to Watch Over Me'.

On round three Richard held out his hand to Morgan, who whispered frantically, 'Richard! I can't dance!'

'Good, you'll encourage everyone else,' he said unsympathetically, and pulled her into his arms.

There was an expectant pause while everyone waited, presumably, for a bravura to match the brilliance of the singer. The band began the introduction for the fourth time. Morgan tripped over Richard's foot, which was in the wrong place.

There was a ripple of laughter as Richard caught her and brought her to her feet again. People began to move onto the floor.

'Richard, I can't do this!' Morgan hissed. 'People are dancing now; let's go back to our seats.'

'Certainly not; we've got to set them a good example. Relax.'

'Ha!' Morgan said bitterly. She realised, when she stopped panicking, that they were shuffling around the floor, an inch or so at a time, in a simple box-step which even she could cope with, while all around them people were doing complicated manoeuvres to the sweet, rich voice of the singer. Why all these Rogers-Astaire dance-alikes had had to remain coyly in their seats while she had been dragged onto the floor remained a mystery.

Her arms crept round Richard's neck, and just for a moment the sweet warmth of the music made her forget that they were enemies, that she'd publicly humiliated him and he was out for revenge. But the firm, relentless pressure of his hands on her waist brought her to earth abruptly. He held her tightly against him, as if they were taking part in the slow dance as lovers, and all the while in the background the flashbulbs popped and whined.

When the music stopped Morgan thought, in a moment of optimism, that she might be allowed to sit down. But no—now a faster piece started up, and Richard whirled her about the dance floor; she was torn between desperate efforts to blunder through the manoeuvres he showed her and bitter, bitter envy of someone who could spend the evening dancing in flat shoes.

Much, much later, when the musicians had gone, and the guests had gone, a few hardy journalists gathered to dig for quotes. They'd filed their stories for the next day, and now they had all the time in the world.

'Do you have plans to marry?'

'What does your sister think?'

'When did you realise you loved each other?'

'How about a kiss for our readers?'

Richard had fielded all questions with aplomb; at the last one, Morgan had the uncomfortable feeling that he'd finally got what he was waiting for.

'Why not?' he said genially, to the astonishment of the journalists. It never hurt to ask, but it didn't usually do much good either.

Richard put one hand on Morgan's shoulder, the other on her jaw, and looked into her eyes. Here we go again, she thought bitterly. Except that she couldn't run far in high-heeled shoes. And she couldn't run anyway, because she'd set this up.

He bent his head closer. If that's how you want it. . . That was what that mocking light in his eyes meant. Morgan gritted her teeth. A few flashes went off too soon. Her eyes met his defiantly.

And then, abruptly, he straightened up and gave an unrepentant shrug to the journalists. 'On second thoughts I think I'll pursue this conversation in private,' he told them. 'You'll have to use your imagination.'

There was a chorus of groans and ribald exclamations. And then Richard strode from the room, dragging Morgan willy-nilly behind him.

Struggling after Richard down the street, then sinking, exhausted, into the passenger seat of his car, Morgan could think of nothing to say. It was only after five or six minutes that she noticed something was wrong. 'You've taken the wrong turning,' she pointed out.

'The hell I have,' he said curtly. 'We're going back to my place.'

'I have nothing to say to you,' she snapped.

'*Good*,' said Richard in a silky tone. 'Because I have quite a lot to say to you.'

And he refused to be drawn further. Morgan briefly considered simply stalking off down the street in search of a night bus as soon as they'd parked. But her feet hurt; she winced at just the thought of walking a mile or so to the nearest bus stop. And anyway, she thought dourly, with Richard in this mood there was no guarantee that he wouldn't just pick her up and carry her back. The result was that she followed him quite meekly into the lift at his block of flats, and walked equally obediently into his flat.

It was only when the door closed quietly behind her and she heard the click of the latch that she wondered whether she'd been a fool.

'All right, let's have this out now,' said Richard.

'Have what out?' Morgan queried uneasily.

'What exactly am I doing wrong?' he asked furiously. 'Is it just that you don't like being told what to do? Or don't like owing me a favour?' He glared down at her, thrusting his hands in his pockets as if he might shake the answer out of her. Oh, she'd got under his skin all right. Somehow it didn't seem so amusing now, tête-à-tête with a well-built, six-foot-tall man in a towering rage.

'As far as I can see,' he added impatiently, 'you actually resent me more *now* than you did when I'd set a bomb under the place. You've been *looking* for something else to seize on as unforgivable, and, my God, I almost handed it to you on a plate!'

Just because he was bigger than she was it didn't mean she had to take this lying down.

'Richard,' Morgan said grittily, 'you are *impossible* to work with. You're impatient, arrogant, unreasonable, and every time you have a brilliant idea it means *I* have to work sixteen hours a day. And you're *always* having brilliant ideas—' She pulled herself up abruptly. '*But*,' she said reluctantly, forcing the words out, 'I'm sorry I gave those interviews. I don't know why I did it. I was just so bloody *tired*. . .' she said helplessly.

'So you blamed me because you played the martyr?' he asked unsympathetically. 'If you couldn't cope with the work we could have got a secretary—'

'We can't afford a secretary,' snapped Morgan. 'You know perfectly well the trustees won't pay for one.'

Richard said something rude under his breath about the trustees. 'How much do you think I make?' he asked impatiently.

Morgan made a wild guess. 'Fifty thousand pounds?' she ventured. After all, media people were ridiculously overpaid.

'About three hundred and fifty thousand pounds a year,' he said coolly. 'Not counting fees for the odd guest appearance. . .'

Morgan gasped. 'You make more than twenty-five thousand pounds a *month*?'

'Disgusting, isn't it? Quite enough to splash out on secretarial assistance if I realise it's needed.'

Morgan stared at him blankly. 'Yes, but, Richard—if you've got all that money, why didn't you just write out a cheque? There was no need for you to turn your life upside down.'

'Why don't you work it out?' he said impatiently.

Morgan opened her mouth. 'Your—' she began.

'And bear in mind that if your next word is "image" it may well be your last,' he added suavely.

'But Elaine said you got a huge post from people who hated the programme,' she protested. 'So naturally I—'

'Naturally you leapt to conclusions.' He struck his head with his hand. 'Morgan, if I took time off work every time someone didn't like a show I'd never see the studio.' He gave her a rather sardonic smile. 'I know you think I'm arrogant; well it's not a business for the thin-skinned, and frankly that kind of thing doesn't keep me awake nights.'

'So you really did like the children?' she hazarded.

'I did and do, but I could have sent them a cheque,' he pointed out. 'And if I did I knew damned well I'd never see you again.'

He began to pace up and down, glancing at her in exasperation from time to time. Morgan had slipped off her shoes—she always took off high-heeled shoes at the first opportunity—and instead of sitting down like any normal woman she now perched on the back of the sofa, long legs dangling loose.

'I should have turned round and headed straight back to London the minute I got my car out of that damned swamp!' he said irritably. 'The whole thing was insane. As soon as you came bouncing out of that damn tyre it was as if something inside said you were the one for me.'

'You were quite appallingly rude when I came bouncing out of that tyre, Richard,' Morgan pointed out.

'And you gave as good as you got, remember?' He grinned reminiscently. 'I couldn't believe my luck when I got up to the house.' His smile faded abruptly, as if he'd suddenly remembered everything that had happened since then.

'I'd never been in love before,' he said simply. 'So I'd no idea what hell it could be.' He grimaced. 'You find someone who lights up a room whenever she comes into it, and it's as if you're bound together by some invisible, unbreakable chain—you have a kind of sixth sense for what she's thinking... And then you find she's done something unforgivable.'

He stopped pacing to pause by the sofa, his face sombre. 'But you can't just walk away and start over again. The bond doesn't break—it just tears you up inside.'

Morgan drew a deep breath. 'But how could you risk destroying the school if you felt that way?'

'I said it was hell, didn't I?' he said grimly. 'I couldn't start playing sordid little games for the first time in my life and just leave Ruth to get on with it. But of course I knew how you'd be bound to feel about it.'

Morgan frowned, searching for something to say. What was she *supposed* to say? Oh, so it hurt you as much as it did me? And then, as if he'd read her thoughts, a gleam of self-mockery lit his face.

'And don't tell me I should have talked to you first,' he added ruefully. 'If I had I'd have realised you could be a useful ally, and I probably *wouldn't* have gone for shock tactics.' A wry smile twisted his mouth. 'I think I was terrified of finding out you'd known all along, so I told myself it was kinder to you to stay away.'

He laughed at her disgusted look. 'Well, I have absolutely no regrets about Ruth; I think she deserved everything she got. But when I heard the charity was still struggling along without her, and *with* you...' He paused, and then admitted with an effort, 'I realised making that programme probably hadn't been the most level-headed move in my career.'

Morgan stared at him. Richard could, as she knew to her cost, be extremely persuasive when he wanted you to think you were irresistibly attractive; if he'd told her that she was beautiful she'd have dismissed it as more of the same old flannel. But for Richard—*Richard*!—to say you'd actually affected his *work*...

He began restlessly pacing again. 'I thought all I had to do was get this damned school on its feet again and everything would be all right. We'd be working together, just the two of us against the world, and, all right, it would be bloody hard work, but I thought you'd have a marvellous time; you'd see I wasn't the monster you'd imagined.

'And instead—' he threw out a hand in sheer exasperation '—you seem to think it's all a sinister design to promote myself at the school's expense, and if you just push me far enough you can trick me into admitting it was all a con.'

Morgan frowned. She'd seen that reckless, clever face confront everything from heads of state to drug barons. And for the first time in four weeks she actually took it in. For *Richard* to walk away from *Firing Line*...! And she'd actually thought it was because of a little bad publicity?

The journalists who'd come tonight could make him look ridiculous—had already had one shot at it—and he'd laughed in their faces. 'You'll have to use your imagination'—in other words, Do your damnedest. The only thing he'd cared about had been the spitefulness which had made her give the interviews. And why had she done it? He'd given her the chance to be part of that sizzling performance, he'd demanded of her the perfection he demanded of himself, and she'd been resentful, and suspicious, and petty.

Morgan slid, wincing, to the ground. 'I—' she began. It was terrifying to think of giving up the safety of hiding her feelings—but, after all, Richard had told her what he felt without any encouragement.

'I've never been in love before either,' she said at last. 'I didn't realise it would be like this. When you did that exposé...' She bit her lip. 'It was just the way you said. It tore me apart. And then, when I saw you again, even though I *knew* what you were like it was just the same—I couldn't look at anyone else in the room.'

He had stopped about three feet away from her. He stood gazing at her, making no move to come closer.

'Richard—' She made a helpless gesture with her hand. 'I know how you feel about *Firing Line*. I don't suppose you'd back down if a *million* viewers hated a programme, never mind a few thousand. But it never occurred to me that you'd do something like that for me.' She looked at him doubtfully. 'I still can't really believe it,' she admitted. 'I keep thinking it must be a joke, to get back at me for those papers—'

Richard said something rude about the papers. Suddenly he was no longer three feet away from her. He rested his hands on the back of the sofa, holding her imprisoned between his arms, and looked down at her.

'Do you mean it, Morgan?' He made it sound like a dare, and Morgan never refused a dare.

'Yes,' she insisted.

Morgan had always thought that it was his predatory eye and cutting wit that had made Richard seem so dangerous. But that was nothing to the danger he conveyed now, not moving an inch closer, his eyes deadly serious, blazing with a combination of tenderness, wild exultation and raw passion.

'So you'll stay with me?'

'Yes,' she said again recklessly. It was lovely not to fight any more. 'Yes, yes, yes, yes, yes.' She laughed suddenly. 'Which was that, anyway?' she said as an afterthought. 'The proposal or the proposition?'

'Both.'

'The answer is still yes.'

CHAPTER TWELVE

MORGAN woke at about ten. Richard was still asleep; there was a strange sweetness to seeing him in this unguarded state, an intimacy as great as those they had shared the night before. She smiled and slipped out of bed; she felt far too full of energy to go back to sleep, and even Richard couldn't be expected to spend the morning making love—not after last night!

She showered and dressed, and had started looking through the paper when she heard the shower start up again. A couple of minutes later the phone began to ring.

Morgan looked at it doubtfully, then strode back into the bedroom.

'Richard!' she bellowed above the shower. 'The telephone's ringing!'

'See what it's about, will you?' came the answering shout. 'Tell them I'll get back to them.'

Morgan returned to the phone in a glow of pleasure; his automatic response as good as said that they belonged together, and he didn't care who knew it. 'Hello?' she said.

'*Morgan*?' said an incredulous voice. 'Is that you?'

'Elaine?'

'My God. I thought you practically weren't on speaking terms. Richard really is amazing.' Her sister's voice was amused.

'He's doing wonderful work for the charity,' Morgan said defensively.

'And this is his reward? Sorry, just joking. I suppose this does mean what I think it does?'

Elaine's tone was exasperating; what did Elaine

know about it? But as Morgan was about to protest a phrase came to her with the sudden, stabbing pain of a poisoned dart. 'Intense but short-lived'. Richard seemed so sincere—but maybe someone sophisticated like Elaine would have a better idea of what that counted for.

'Well, we spent the night together. . .' she admitted.

'Well, good for you, Morgan; it's about time you started living a little more adventurously,' said Elaine jauntily. 'And what better place to start than Richard?'

'It wasn't like that,' Morgan protested. 'He says he wants me to marry him.'

There was a short silence. 'I see,' said Elaine.

'I—I think he means it,' said Morgan. 'But I don't know anyone like him, Elaine. He thinks he wants to spend the rest of his life with me, but I just wonder whether having all those girlfriends wouldn't be a sort of habit.'

Elaine sighed. 'Morgan, I think you should be very, very careful. If he means it there may be more to this than meets the eye—I've always heard Richard stood to come into some huge trust fund on the birth of his first child, and most of the women he knows wouldn't necessarily plan to present him with a *petit paquet* nine months after the wedding. That may have started to weigh with him—that's *if* he means it.'

'Is that really what you think?'

'I don't know,' said Elaine. 'Journalism makes you pretty cynical. I wouldn't have said Richard was the marrying type, somehow.' She hesitated. 'It's just possible, you know, that he actually set out to make you fall for him, after all those things you said. . . Morgan, don't hate me for asking this, but did he mention marriage before or after you'd slept together?'

'Before.'

There was a very long silence. 'Morgan,' Elaine said at last, 'try not to let your emotions get too involved in this, OK? I could be completely wrong,' she admitted, 'but I think you'd do better just to enjoy this for what it is, you know? After all, he really is something pretty special in bed, whatever one may think about him personally.'

Morgan sank down heavily on a chair. 'Do you mean you—?'

'We spent some time together when he was handing over *Firing Line*,' Elaine explained fluently. 'Well, you know what it's like; you're working late, have a few drinks—good way to relax, hmm? Just don't take it seriously; I'm afraid he'll always be a bit of a lad; some men are like that.'

'Oh,' said Morgan.

Elaine dropped the subject. 'Actually, what I called about was just to firm up some arrangements about a joint feature on this work he's been doing—'

'What, about A Child's Place?' asked Morgan uneasily.

'Well, yes, of course about winding that down, but more about the big boys. I think he's right, don't you? From what I understand, fund-raising and admin at A Child's Place is hideously expensive for what it is; far better for all the eggs to go in a big basket...' She paused. 'Sweet of Richard to give me a nibble for old times' sake,' she added.

'Wasn't it just?' said Morgan. 'I'll tell him you called,' she said dully.

She put the phone down. She wished desperately that she'd said nothing to Elaine—except that, if what Elaine had said was true, Morgan's not knowing wouldn't have changed anything. She tried to think herself back into her mood of happy confidence; Elaine hadn't seen his face—why should Elaine be right? But he'd obviously been doing *something* behind her back—why should she believe anything he said?

The sound of water next door was cut off and

Richard emerged from the bedroom, energetically drying his hair, his long, lean body still gleaming from the shower. Morgan braced herself for questions about the phone call, but he seemed to have forgotten all about it. His eyes caught hers across the room and he came towards her and put his arms round her, holding her against his warm, damp body. He kissed her lingeringly, and in spite of herself Morgan melted against him.

'I—I need to go back to my place and change,' she said presently, sounding forced and artificial even to herself.

'All a bit overwhelming, isn't it?' He smiled down at her. 'Well, it might do us good to have a breathing space of a few hours. All right if I come round at four?'

Morgan nodded. She needed time to think.

She took a bus home, and got back at about twelve. She kicked her shoes into a corner, tossed her dress onto the bed, and put on a faded red T-shirt, a pair of very baggy, very soft old khaki trousers and her ancient, blissfully comfortable white plimsolls. She needed to think. She needed to say something to Richard.

By four, when his car drew up outside, she still hadn't thought of anything. She heard his feet come bounding down the path; she opened the door and he swept her into his arms, kissing her until her head spun. Then he stepped back to look at her, and his face creased into one of those irresistible smiles. 'Don't you just hate it when your coach turns into a pumpkin?' he asked.

Morgan smiled rather wanly.

'Just teasing—you look wonderful. What shall we do? It's too early to eat; do you want to go for a drive or see a film? Or we could stay here and try fifty positions never before achieved in a single bed—' If

Morgan hadn't known better, she'd have thought that he was drunk.

He pulled her into his arms again, his mouth against her hair. 'God, I've missed you. It's only been five hours and it feels like years... I started wondering whether it was too early to leave about twenty minutes after you'd left.' And then his mouth was on hers again. It was impossible that she should ask any of the things on her mind.

Presently they went into the sitting room. 'Elaine called you,' said Morgan, her heart beating faster.

'Oh, yes? And what did she have to say?' he asked in a tone of perfect indifference. Surely it couldn't be true? He *couldn't* talk like that if he had a guilty conscience, could he? But then perhaps he wouldn't think it was something to feel guilty about.

'She wanted to firm arrangements about some programme—'

'I'll give her a ring on Monday. She didn't happen to say how the show was going?'

'No,' said Morgan. She hesitated, and found that she was back in his arms. He sank onto a sofa, pulling her down to his lap, and began kissing her again. The strength of his arms around her, the solid power of his body, the persuasive sweetness of his kisses at first made her dismiss her doubts as madness—but then he had kissed Elaine too. She had seen him.

'Richard,' she said at last, when he had paused for breath and was tugging gently at the end of her plait, a rather quizzical smile on his mouth. 'Richard, did you— did you and Elaine ever sleep together?' she blurted out.

'Good Lord, have you been worrying about that? No—I'd always fancied her in a fairly unurgent kind of way when I used to see her around the studio, but, of course, as soon as I saw her crazy sister...' The warmth in his eyes completed the sentence.

'But you kissed her,' said Morgan. 'Before dinner that first night. And when you came up to your room.'

He frowned in recollection. '*Did* I? Oh, hang on, I do remember—well, I'd have said she kissed me, which is slightly different, don't you think? I'm not saying I put up a fight—we'd have both looked right fools if I had, seems to me. I can't see myself putting on a very convincing performance of outraged virtue, somehow.'

'Elaine said you did.'

'Did what?'

'Sleep with her.'

There. She'd said it. Now she wished the ground would just open and swallow her. Because now that look was back—that old look of fierce concentration, of puzzling out something that did not make sense.

He raised an eyebrow with faint irony. 'How embarrassing. Now if only you'd told me that in the first place, instead of asking whether we had, I wouldn't have been caught out contradicting a lady. Damn.'

Morgan tried to rally her forces. It wasn't easy because the problem was that he was right—if he *hadn't* done anything, then it was she who was guilty of the most horrible treachery by even *thinking* of believing Elaine. But even if she was in the wrong she wouldn't be a treacherous doormat.

'Don't be sarcastic, Richard. I wasn't trying to trip you up. It's just... I admit it bothered me, but I couldn't think how to bring it up. What do you want me to say? By the way, Elaine was just saying how marvellous you are in bed—I'd no idea you were that close? Or was I supposed to keep it to myself so as not to bother you?'

'No, of course not.' He ran his hand absently up and down her back, offering some kind of reassurance that he still liked her. His eyes met hers. 'Sorry. It's just that this makes me nervous. Elaine and I obviously have different versions of what happened; well, all I can do is to say again that we were never involved. If you don't trust me there's no reason why you should believe me, and something about the line of questioning tells me you don't trust me very much. I obviously can't make you trust me by saying nothing happened, so. . .'

He shrugged. 'I've never denied that I've had other lovers. I haven't even asked you about yours; I just assumed that you felt the way I did—that you'd never met someone you wanted to spend your life with. Morgan, darling, can't you believe I love you? I'd rather be with you than anyone else—yes, even now I'd rather be here than anywhere else, because you're here—even if it means arguing about something completely preposterous.'

His lips brushed hers. Morgan put her arms round his neck. He groaned. 'All I want is to get married as soon as possible,' he said in her ear. 'Can education secretaries marry people? We could get it thrown in with the award at the House of Commons do, before I go back to *Firing Line*.'

Morgan stiffened. She sat up slightly. 'Do you want children?' she asked huskily. She could never have imagined that she would so dread an affirmative answer.

'I don't know; is *The Little Mermaid* compulsory?' he asked flippantly. 'That is, I suppose I'd taken it for granted we would, though when I think of the pack of daredevils we'll produce between us my heart does rather fail me. Perhaps we should stop at one. Or do you think the silver spoon is too big for just one little mouth?'

'I don't know,' said Morgan. 'Was it—was it for you? Do you want it back now?'

Something in her tone caught his ear. He raised an eyebrow again. 'Am I marrying you for my money, do you mean? No. Is that another of Elaine's little ideas?'

Morgan avoided his eye.

'You know,' he remarked thoughtfully, 'if I'd realised Elaine had this penchant for tabloid journalism I wouldn't have been nearly so keen to have her on the show. I can't believe you took this seriously.'

He raised an eyebrow. 'To tell the truth, I wasn't giving much thought to how soon I could get you pregnant after the wedding. I was rather looking forward, after the usual tests and a reasonable interval, to discarding plastic contraception—but then perhaps you wouldn't be too happy about that. After all, who's to say what I might get up to?'

Morgan sprang to her feet. 'I'm sorry,' she said. 'I'm sorry. But don't you see, Richard? Of *course* I didn't believe it. I kept thinking of all the things you'd said to me, and how you'd looked, and how you'd touched me, and I thought it couldn't possibly be true.'

Her grey eyes were steady. 'But that's just what I thought last time. When I saw you with the children—when I thought of what you were like with me—I thought you could never do anything to harm A Child's Place. But you did. How can I possibly know what you think is right?'

She began pacing slowly up and down the room, hands in her pockets. 'If it makes you feel any better,' she said sombrely, 'I'm sure you wouldn't do anything you thought was wrong. But how on earth am I to know what you would count?' Maybe he wouldn't even count winding the place down—not even now.

'I see.' His face was grim. 'So are you saying you'd like to call it off, or you need to think some more, or what?'

Tell me about this new scheme without being forced into it. Tell me something you don't have to because you've been found out... Morgan stared at him silently, willing him to speak.

'You don't know.' He locked his hands behind his

head, considering. 'I think it was a mistake to bring all this up with so much still in the air,' he said at last.

And whose fault was that? Morgan tried to work up a sense of injury at the unfairness of it all, but she couldn't. The contrast between Richard's earlier exuberance and this controlled, businesslike manner was horrible.

'Let's just say "as you were", as far as that's possible, until after the thing at the House of Commons,' he said calmly. 'It's a tricky thing to organise, and we can't really afford to be distracted by emotional ups and downs. And who knows?' He gave a rather sardonic grin. 'Maybe by then you'll feel you know me a bit better.'

CHAPTER THIRTEEN

'I DON'T know if that's such a good idea, Elaine.'

Morgan froze on the stairs outside Richard's office, clutching biscuits and two mugs of coffee that she'd brought up from the pantry.

'I mean, I know it would be great TV, but I don't think it would do my career much good to throttle you on the air... You know damned well what I'm talking about. What on earth possessed you to tell Morgan we'd had an affair?'

There was a very long silence. Morgan stood motionless, two mugs of coffee cooling rapidly in her right hand, a packet of digestives wilting in her left.

At last Richard spoke again, and now his voice was quite different—wary. 'Yes, of course I'm still interested. Wednesday next week? Yes, I think I can manage that; OK, see you then.'

Morgan heard the receiver being replaced in its cradle. She crept into her office, poured tepid coffee into a pot plant, and walked noisily back downstairs with the empty mugs. She returned in a moment or two, and took a cup in to Richard.

He raised his eyes to hers. 'I've never lied to you, Morgan,' he said gravely. 'Can't you believe that?'

Morgan felt a sudden spurt of anger. Hadn't she just heard him talking to Elaine? 'You can be economical with the truth when it suits you, though,' she said coldly. 'I don't remember hearing about your plans for A Child's Place before you dropped the bombshell about Ruth on your programme. And now it seems you've decided to close it down without bothering to tell me anything about it.'

'What?'

'Isn't that what you're going to talk to Elaine about?' she insisted.

Anger flared up in his eyes. 'Of *course*,' he retorted. 'Now that I've raised a quarter of a million for the place I thought it would be fun to pull the plug. After all,' he added silkily, 'why stick around when I've satisfied my curiosity?'

'Hiding behind sarcasm, Richard?' Morgan kicked this red herring ruthlessly aside. 'If there's nothing wrong, why didn't you tell me about it?'

'Because it's delicate and confidential,' he replied impatiently. 'You'll just have to assume I know what I'm doing and can be trusted.'

'Since you've behaved with such integrity so far,' said Morgan nastily. Couldn't he see how badly he'd behaved? 'I think we have different ideas about the sort of openness marriage involves,' she added relentlessly. 'Why don't we just go back to a professional relationship? Then you can do whatever you like.'

'Fine.' His face suddenly impassive, Richard stood up and reached for his coat.

'Where are you going?' she asked. Why wouldn't he stay and fight?

His face was closed, angry. 'Home,' he said. 'It's five o'clock. Office hours are over.' He strode past her, coat slung over his shoulder. At the door he paused, with his old, infuriating instinct for timing. 'I don't know whether you care about my plans now, but I wouldn't want you to think I was hiding anything from you,' he said sardonically. 'I expect I'll pick up at *Firing Line* again as soon as the HOC do is over.'

His footsteps retreated down the stairs.

Morgan squared her shoulders. All right, she couldn't rely on Richard. But she could still rely on herself. She crossed the landing, and went back to work.

* * *

She had plenty of time to get used to solitary late nights. Richard continued to leave on the dot of five every day—more often than not, it seemed, to meet Elaine—and except for the odd 'networking' evening when she still joined him she had the place to herself.

Morgan had had three weeks of this lonely existence when Richard came into her office just before five one day.

'I may be late for this thing tonight,' he told her. 'I'm seeing Elaine; I'm not sure how long it will take.'

'Fine,' said Morgan. She had already changed; the long-sleeved black velvet dress with its wide, shallow boat-neck and narrow skirt gave her a look—she hoped—vaguely reminiscent of Audrey Hepburn: elegant, charming, an irresistible ambassador for a good cause. Her arms were perhaps more muscular than was really suitable for willowy grace, but the long sleeves should take care of that.

He looked down at her, his dark, charismatic face inscrutable. She *knew* what he was like—so why, she thought with something like despair, did her heart still beat faster as soon as he entered the room?

'You look beautiful,' he said.

'I don't need you to tell me that!' Morgan snapped.

'And they say there's no such thing as progress,' he murmured. 'Well, I'll see you on the barricades.'

They had been invited to a picnic-cum-concert in a large country house on the outskirts of London. Morgan had stopped being surprised by the things to which people were expected to wear evening dress; of *course*, men in black tie and women in grand frocks were trying to find ways not to sit on damp grass. By rights, having arrived separately, she shouldn't have seen Richard all evening—he should have been indistinguishable from a hundred or so other men in penguin suits. But of *course*, of *course* she knew the instant he came; knew who was at the centre of a ripple in the crowd even before she saw him.

The crowd parted and she saw him, tossing out greetings, scanning faces. Well, she knew who he was looking for, and just for an instant she longed to run forward over the grass. But then what? He would tell her more of the same old lies, knowing how desperately she wanted to believe him. . .

Suddenly Morgan could bear it no longer. Why was she wasting time here? She couldn't talk about the charity over the music; she might just as well go home. No—she might just as well go straight back to the school and do something useful for a change.

It was about eleven when Morgan got off the bus in Limehouse. This was the first time she'd come back to the office so late, though she'd left later than this, and she felt slightly uneasy as she picked her way along the pavement. But, after all, there was nothing to keep anyone lurking in this little back street, she assured herself, and she unlocked the front door and let herself in. She bolted the door behind her, made herself an instant coffee, and limped upstairs.

For the next three hours a single upstairs light gleamed out over the dark little street while Morgan worked her way through her letters. It was no doubt a tribute to Richard's success that there were more of these than ever. At two a.m. she printed out the last letter, put letters in envelopes, franked the envelopes with the new day's date, and put a satisfyingly substantial bundle in the 'Post Out' box.

She stretched and sighed, then turned out the light and made her way downstairs. She would go home and take off her shoes, she promised herself.

She stepped out into the dark street, closing the door behind her. As she made her way to the road a figure stepped away from the wall at the corner, silhouetted from behind by the dim streetlight.

'Excuse me,' he said. 'I wonder if you can help me?'

'I don't think so,' said Morgan. He began to walk towards her. She turned and began to hurry in the opposite direction, hearing his footsteps break into a run behind her. Gritting her teeth, she put on speed—and then her foot turned on an uneven stone and she was down. An arm closed round her neck and a heavy weight collapsed on her from behind.

Suddenly Morgan lost her self-control. She'd been forced to say nice things about Richard to a crowd of glittering strangers when she wanted to tell them what a swine he was. For *weeks* she'd had to be polite to Richard instead of giving him the black eye he so richly deserved. Well, enough was enough. Her assailant found his arms round an explosion of flailing heels and elbows; sharp teeth closed on his wrist. And when he tried to shift his grasp his prey rolled over, and now knees and fists came into play as Morgan made sure that at least *somebody* got a black eye.

There was a growl of rage. They were grappling in the shadow of a wall, cut off from the light by a line of rubbish bins; neither could see to fight effectively. Morgan's problem was that unless she knocked him out she couldn't get away—she couldn't run on her high heels and she couldn't leave them behind to run on that glass-littered street.

She kept grabbing his head, trying to knock it against something—but half the time the only things to get knocked were her knuckles, which kept getting banged and scraped on the cement. And then she heard footsteps tearing down the street.

In the heat of the fight her first thought was that an accomplice had come to back up her assailant. The first man slackened his efforts at the noise, obviously expecting reinforcements. Then suddenly he wasn't there, and a new, taller figure bent over her. Morgan sprang up, giving her best right jab; the figure flinched backwards.

'Damn it, Morgan, it's me,' said Richard. 'You little hell-cat, I think you've just given me a black eye.'

'*Good*,' said Morgan, who had lost most of her inhibitions. Her heart was beating like a sledgehammer and she was breathing hoarsely. 'Where is he?' she asked ferociously.

'Over there; I knocked him out. Are you all right?'

'Of course I'm all right.' Morgan hobbled over to the limp body of her foe; one of her heels seemed to have got broken in the fray. 'Damn you, Richard, *I* was going to knock him out,' she said ungratefully. 'I was *winning*. I can look after myself; there was absolutely no need for you to interfere.'

'Oh, for God's sake—' He bit back whatever he had been planning to add to this and said, with strong self-control, 'We'll talk about that later, shall we? Let's get rid of him first—there must be a police station somewhere nearby.'

'I think there's one on East India Dock Road,' said Morgan. 'Anyway, you knocked him out so he's all yours—you can get him to the car.'

She tried, unsuccessfully, not to be impressed by the ease with which Richard hoisted the man over his shoulder, and limped by his side to the main road, where his car was parked. Under Richard's instructions she removed his keys from his pocket to open the car, and lowered a seat so that the body could be wedged in the back.

'What are you doing here, anyway?' she asked. 'It's the middle of the night.'

There was a short, pregnant silence. 'Yes,' said Richard. 'I'm glad you noticed that. It *is* the middle of the night, when only thieves, muggers, rapists and your sweet, mad self are abroad. You bloody *fool*—' He got into the driver's seat and slammed the door shut.

Morgan got into the passenger's seat, a riposte on her lips—but he was in full flow again.

'I wanted to talk to you, so I called you when I got back. I was a bit worried when there was no answer, but of course services aren't so regular at that time of night. I kept calling about every fifteen minutes or so until twelve-thirty, when I realised it couldn't possibly have taken you that long to get home. I started imagining all kinds of ghastly accidents—and then it occurred to me that it might just have seemed a clever idea to you to pop into the office for a few hours. So I called, but that damned answering machine was on. . .

'At first I thought I'd just wait until tomorrow to talk to you, but finally I couldn't stand it any longer, so I came down here. Sorry my timing was off; if I'd waited a few minutes longer you could have had all the fun yourself.'

The car was bolting down the deserted streets, past shops protected by iron grilles and corrugated-iron shutters. At last it pulled up abruptly outside the police station, whose light shone unflatteringly on wild hair, a scratched and bruised face, and torn clothes smeared with rotting vegetables.

'Don't you know any better than to go out dressed like that at that time of night down that kind of street?' he snapped. 'It's asking for trouble—'

Morgan had begun to open her door, but at this she turned and glared at him. 'It is not; statistically, far more women are raped in their *homes* by people they *know*, which means that I could be running a much *greater* risk spending a quiet evening in my own flat with *you*.'

She got out and slammed the door. She watched, without offering to help, while Richard struggled to extract the now stirring body from the back seat.

'And anyway,' she added unanswerably, 'you're a fine one to talk about asking for trouble. Some people might think it was asking for trouble to waltz into a guerrilla hideout with a camcorder and beg to differ with the leader on the subject of land redistribution, but that didn't stop you, did it? *Some* people might think it wasn't such a good idea to parachute into a rebel enclave armed only with an out-of-date mission-ary phrasebook for a related dialect. *Some people* might think it wasn't exactly the height of prudence to quiz the head of a drug cartel about the morality of drug trafficking.

'But then some people,' she concluded sarcastically, 'haven't met daredevils like me who work late at the office.'

Richard threw her a look so furious that she was momentarily cowed. She followed him, somewhat sub-dued, into the police station, and then quietly seethed when the duty sergeant assumed that all the credit for her assailant's poor condition was due to Richard.

'Lucky for you the gentleman came along,' he remarked reproachfully. It was then Richard's turn to fume while Morgan made out a lengthy statement which seemed to consist largely of 'He tried to tear my dress. I struck him on the eye. He tried to gag me. I bit his hand. I was on the point of knocking him uncon-scious when Mr Kavanagh arrived'.

At length Richard stalked out again, Morgan limping behind him.

'Now what?' said Morgan.

'Get in,' he said curtly. 'I'm taking you home. I want to talk to you.'

'How do I know you won't attack me?'

'You don't.' He glared at her. 'What does it take to shake some sense into you? We're going back to your place and I'm not leaving until you promise never to do anything like this again.'

'Don't hold your breath,' said Morgan, glaring back. 'I shall do exactly as I please, starting now. *I* shall take

the night bus home; *you* can drive your car elsewhere.
You take the high road and I take the low road. Why
should you care what I do? You're about to go back to
Firing Line and ogle my sister on a weekly basis in
front of millions of viewers.' She turned on her one
good heel and began to limp down the street, but she
was stopped after two strides by his hand on her arm.

'Morgan,' he said in a tone of deadly calm. 'What
you do with the rest of your life is your business. If you
want to put up a notice outside the door—"At Home
to the Criminal Classes after two a.m., Martial Arts
Our Speciality"—there's nothing I can do to stop you.
But tonight you are going home in my car, and you're
going to let me check the doors and windows, because
I'm damned if I'm going to lie awake wondering if
some other piece of low life had better luck.'

Morgan would have liked to say something incisive
about the piece of low life on the pavement beside her
but suddenly she felt very weary. The fight must have
tired her out more than she'd realised. She shook off
his hand and walked back to the car.

She'd expected more remonstrances on her folly, but
Richard was perfectly silent as the car wove through
the dark streets. He pulled up outside her house in
about twenty minutes and got out of the car. Morgan
did the same. She thought of pointing out that an attack
outside her office didn't make it any likelier that an
intruder would break into her flat, but one look at
Richard's grim face told her that she'd be wasting her
breath.

He followed her into the flat. Morgan closed the
door behind him. 'Well, do you want to have a look
round?' she asked.

'In a moment,' he said. And suddenly his arms were
around her, wrapped so tightly behind her back that
she could hardly breathe. For a long time he stood
holding her, not speaking, his head against her hair.

'Thank God you're safe,' he said at last. One hand stroked her hair. 'Thank God you're all right.' His arms loosened slightly, and he raised his head to look into her face. His eyes seemed to widen in their steady, relentless gaze, as if to take in all at once every detail of something indescribably precious which he might have lost for ever.

Under that serious look Morgan felt a tight knot of misery dissolving inside her; wrapped in his arms, pinned by his gaze, suddenly she did feel safe—safe from a loss so terrible that she hadn't been able to admit to being afraid of it.

'Richard,' she said softly, her low, husky voice making it sound like a caress. She leant her cheek against his chest.

They stood that way for a very long time, neither wanting to move. At last Morgan said reluctantly, not moving, 'I should get cleaned up...' And then she added, in horror, 'Oh, Richard! Now I've got this all over you!' She pulled his arms apart and stepped back, and looked in dismay at the once immaculate dinner suit, now smeared with the unspeakable muck from the gutter.

He glanced down, a smile tugging at the corner of his mouth. 'Well, this really is like old times, isn't it?' he said. 'Don't tell me, you'll have it cleaned—'

'I'm not sure it *will* come out, to tell the truth,' said Morgan. 'But I do love you.'

'And I love you.'

Morgan sighed and gave him a bitter-sweet smile. 'I'll just shower and I'll be right out.'

She slipped into the bathroom to strip off her torn and dirty dress, showering quickly, and in a few minutes was out again, a white terry dressing gown wrapped around her, her black hair streaming straight down her back like wet silk.

She found Richard in the sitting room. He had

discarded his jacket—probably for good—and was leaning against the back of the sofa. The white dress shirt, the black trousers with their satin side-stripe seemed a civilised veneer on a body which could be a lethal fighting weapon; they couldn't quite conceal the powerful muscles of the broad shoulders, the long, lean legs they clothed.

She hadn't thought that she'd made a noise, but he seemed to sense her at the door. He looked up, still with that warm, glowing look, and stretched out an arm as if inviting her to come inside it. Morgan crossed the room and leant against his side while his arm curled round her.

'Richard?'

'Yes?'

'Maybe I couldn't have knocked him out. Thank you.'

'Any time.' There was a short pause. 'I still think you were insane to be down there, but let's leave that for later... There's quite a lot I've got to tell you. First of all, is your heart really set on A Child's Place having administrative autonomy? If you could have a guarantee that the school would go on just as it is now, under the auspices of a larger organisation, would you really mind?'

Morgan shook her head. 'I don't know...'

'I've been talking to Dan Sharmutt at Overhead, and they're willing to take it on.' His hand lightly stroked her arm. 'Morgan—I've never forgotten those classes I saw. There you were, in a bare room with a bit of paper and a few pencils and those crazy kids, and they weren't just learning something, they were having a marvellous time. I've never seen anything like it.

'If Overhead take over you could go back to that straight away, whereas if the charity takes on a new complement of staff for admin... Well, it's in better

nick than it was a couple of months ago, but they'll
have an uphill battle. . .'

'No, it's a good idea,' said Morgan. 'Was that what. . .
was that what Elaine meant when she said you were
winding it down?' she asked gruffly.

'Well,' said Richard, 'I don't suppose it was what she
meant you to think.' The grey eyes glittered with barely
suppressed exasperation. 'It seems Elaine was worried
about my intentions. She thought you were getting too
emotionally involved. So just when I'd finally managed
to persuade you you'd misjudged me she threw a
spanner in the works. She thought it would be better to
let you think I'd slept with her, and maybe even that I
was sabotaging A Child's Place, before things went any
further.'

'She *what*?'

'So I told her I loved you, and she thought it was
hilarious. She said I'd have my hands full and serve me
right.'

'Naturally it didn't occur to either of you that I might
be interested,' Morgan said sarcastically.

'I made her promise not to tell.' Just fleetingly the
arrogant, black-browed face looked *almost* remorseful.
'Don't be too angry with her, will you? She meant it
for the best, and if it hadn't been for Elaine I wouldn't
be here tonight.'

The brilliant eyes scanned her face, the familiar
gleam of amusement lighting the hard features. 'I was
pretty furious that you hadn't trusted me,' he said
ruefully. 'I was damned if I'd go on throwing myself at
your feet just so you could look down your nose at me;
I couldn't understand why you found it so incredible
that I could love you.

'But Elaine told me a bit more about your mother. . .
I remember you once told me some story about her
and she sounded quite a character, but I hadn't realised

the family verdict was that she was someone no man
could be expected to live with!'

'I don't think that—'

'You don't think someone like Elaine is what every
man is looking for in his heart of hearts?'

'Well—'

'Morgan,' Richard said sweetly, 'do you know what
I'd like to read in the papers fifty years from now?'

'WORLD AT PEACE—IT'S OFFICIAL?'

'PLUCKY GRAN ABSEILS OFF TELECOM TOWER.'

Morgan gave a crack of laughter.

'"I never refuse a dare," said Mrs Kavanagh,' he
continued solemnly. 'The fey, gamine, hauntingly beautiful, Hepburn/Garbo/Dietrich look-alike, slim seventy-
six-year-old is celebrating her golden wedding anniver-
sary. Asked to comment on his wife's exploit, media
tycoon Richard Kavanagh expressed himself in colourful but unprintable language.'

'Censorship is such a nuisance,' Morgan murmured.

He grinned. 'What I'm saying is that what I want is
you. You'll drive me insane, but I'd rather be insane
with you than sane without you. I don't want some
other woman you might pretend to be. I don't want to
try you out as flavour of the month. I want you.'

'And you always get what you want sooner or
later. . .'

'Naturally.' There was a glint in his eye. 'Or I would
if you'd just realise that, since I find you irresistible,
you don't have to be so damned suspicious because you
feel the same way about me.'

'I do not find you—' Morgan began, but she was cut
off as he kissed her with a thoroughness that left her in
no doubt about his feelings. Much, much later, when
her response had, she realised, made it pointless to
continue that particular sentence, he raised his head
and gave her another of those maddening, irresistible
smiles.

'What's the dare?' asked Morgan, faint but pursuing.
'To put up with you for fifty years?'

He laughed out loud. Arrogant, exasperating, over-bearing...and, Morgan realised, her defences crumbling, completely addictive.

'If anyone can do it,' he told her, 'you can.'

It occurred to Morgan that she still hadn't beaten Richard at his own game. It was going to take a bit longer than she'd expected. In fact, quite a lot longer...

'All right,' she said, eyes sparkling in anticipation. 'I accept.'

MILLS & BOON

**For those long, hot, lazy days this summer
Mills & Boon are delighted to bring you...**

**A collection of four short sizzling stories
in one romantic volume.**

We know you'll love these warm and sensual
stories from some of our best loved authors.

Love Me Not	Barbara Stewart
Maggie And Her Colonel	Merline Lovelace
Prairie Summer	Alina Roberts
Anniversary Waltz	Anne Marie Duquette

'Stolen Moments' is the perfect summer read for
those stolen summer moments!

Available: June '96   Price: £4.99

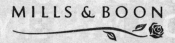

MILLS & BOON

Back by Popular Demand

BETTY
NEELS

COLLECTOR'S EDITION

**A collector's edition of favourite titles
from one of the world's best-loved
romance authors.**

Mills & Boon are proud to bring back these
sought after titles, now reissued in beautifully
matching volumes and presented as one
cherished collection.

Don't miss these unforgettable titles, coming
next month:

Title #3   A GENTLE AWAKENING
Title #4   RING IN A TEACUP

Available wherever
Mills & Boon books are sold

GET 4 BOOKS
AND A MYSTERY GIFT

Return this coupon and we'll send you 4 Mills & Boon Romances and a mystery gift absolutely FREE! We'll even pay the postage and packing for you.

We're making you this offer to introduce you to the benefits of Reader Service: FREE home delivery of brand-new Mills & Boon Romances, at least a month before they are available in the shops, FREE gifts and a monthly Newsletter packed with information.

Accepting these FREE books and gift places you under no obligation to buy, you may cancel at any time, even after receiving just your free shipment. Simply complete the coupon below and send it to:

MILLS & BOON READER SERVICE, FREEPOST, CROYDON, SURREY, CR9 3WZ.

No stamp needed

Yes, please send me 4 free Mills & Boon Romances and a mystery gift. I understand that unless you hear from me, I will receive 6 superb new titles every month for just £2.10* each postage and packing free. I am under no obligation to purchase any books and I may cancel or suspend my subscription at any time, but the free books and gifts will be mine to keep in any case. (I am over 18 years of age)

1EP6R

Ms/Mrs/Miss/Mr _____

Address _____

_____

_____ Postcode _____

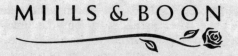

MILLS & BOON

Next Month's Romances

Each month you can choose from a wide variety of romance with Mills & Boon. Below are the new titles to look out for next month.

ONLY BY CHANCE	Betty Neels
THE MORNING AFTER	Michelle Reid
THE DESERT BRIDE	Lynne Graham
THE RIGHT CHOICE	Catherine George
FOR THE LOVE OF EMMA	Lucy Gordon
WORKING GIRL	Jessica Hart
THE LADY'S MAN	Stephanie Howard
THE BABY BUSINESS	Rebecca Winters
WHITE LIES	Sara Wood
THAT MAN CALLAHAN!	Catherine Spencer
FLIRTING WITH DANGER	Kate Walker
THE BRIDE'S DAUGHTER	Rosemary Gibson
SUBSTITUTE ENGAGEMENT	Jayne Bauling
NOT PART OF THE BARGAIN	Susan Fox
THE PERFECT MAN	Angela Devine
JINXED	Day Leclaire